FOREVER
NINETEEN

FOREVER NINETEEN

GRIGORY BAKLANOV

translated by Antonina W. Bouis

J. B. LIPPINCOTT   NEW YORK

Forever Nineteen
Text copyright © 1979 by Oktiabr Magazine
English translation copyright © 1989 by Antonina W. Bouis
First published under the title *Naveki—deviatnadtsatiletnie*
by Grigory Baklanov.

1   2   3   4   5   6   7   8   9   10
First American Edition

Library of Congress Cataloging-in-Publication Data
Baklanov, Grigorii IAkovlevich.
    [Naveki—deviatnadtsatiletnie.   English]
    Forever nineteen / by Grigory Baklanov ; translated by Antonina W.
Bouis.
        p.   cm.
    Translation of: Naveki—deviatnadtsatiletnie.
    Summary: The experiences of a nineteen-year-old Soviet lieutenant
on the front during World War II as he defends his Russian homeland
from the Nazis.
    ISBN 0-397-32296-8 : $. — ISBN 0-397-32297-6 (lib. bdg.) ;
$
    1. World War, 1939-1945—Soviet Union—Fiction. [1. World War,
1939-1945—Soviet Union—Fiction.   2. Soviet Union—Fiction.]
I. Title.
PG3476.B28635N313   1989   88-26622
891.73′44—dc19   CIP
[Fic]   AC

AUTHOR'S NOTE

I recently received a letter from the United States from a reader of my book *The Foothold*. It was published about thirty years ago in England, and it described the invasion of our country by the Nazi army and the battles beyond the Dniester River. The American who read the book wrote to tell me that if he had to be in a war now, he would like to be in the same foxhole with my book's hero.

But Americans and Russians *were* practically in the same foxhole in World War II. We were allies. We fought for the same goal. The victory over fascism was our joint victory. And soldiers from our armies met at the Elbe River and shook hands. They were young men. Now they are far from young, they have children and grandchildren—a lot of time has passed since then. But the ones who did not live to see the victory, who gave their lives for it, they have remained forever young. This book is about them, about their youth, their love, their sacred faith.

I was seventeen and finishing high school when the war broke out. We had twenty boys and twenty girls in our class. Almost all the boys went to the front, but I was the only one to return alive. Our city, Voronezh, the ancient Russian city of the steppes, perished under the bombs, was destroyed by the artillery, and was blown up by the Germans when they retreated. I came back after the war, in the winter of 1946. None of my family was there. My two older brothers had been killed—one near Moscow in 1941, the other in the Ukraine.

I looked up a former classmate, and she and I went out to the only surviving restaurant in the city. Heavy snow fell outside the windows. I watched it fall across the street into our old apartment through the collapsed roof, onto the smashed beams and floors, through the iron supports of the balcony. My whole life had been spent in that house.

Voronezh has been rebuilt, and now there are twice as many people living there, but the city we knew and loved is alive only in our memory. And only in our memory are people who no longer exist still alive and still young. I wanted them to come alive when I wrote this book. I wanted people living now to care about them as friends, as family, as brothers.

I am glad that this book, which has been translated into many languages, is being published in the United States. I hope you will find the people in it dear to you. They are part of our people, who lived through the most horrible of wars and who, just like the American people, want peace above all.

Grigory Baklanov

FOREVER
NINETEEN

1

The living stood at the edge of the trench. He was inside. Nothing about him that in life distinguishes one person from another had survived. It was impossible to tell who he had been: one of our soldiers? a German? But the teeth were young and strong.

The shovel struck something—a belt buckle, oxidized green and packed with sand, with a star on it. They passed it around carefully. It told them he was one of ours, most likely an officer.

It began to rain. The rain pattered on the backs and shoulders of the military shirts the actors were wearing to break in before the filming began. The battles in this area had taken place over thirty years ago, before many of these people were born, and for all those years he had lain in the trench. Spring waters and rains had seeped down to him in the ground and were sucked out again by the roots of trees and grasses. Now the rain was washing him. Drops dripped from his dark eye sockets, leaving topsoil traces; water poured along the exposed collarbones, the wet ribs, washing away sand and dirt from places where lungs had once breathed and a heart had beaten. The young teeth, wet in the rain, took on a lifelike glistening.

"Cover him with a cape," the director said. He had brought his crew here to make a movie about World War II and they were digging new trenches where the old ones, long ago filled in and covered with grass, had been.

Workmen stretched out a cape and made a tent. The summer rain banged on it, seeming to come down harder. The sun was shining, and steam rose from the earth. After a rain like that, all living things spurt into growth.

That night stars shone brightly across the entire sky. As he had over thirty years ago, he lay in an open trench. The August stars above tore away from their spots and fell, leaving bright trails in the sky. In the morning the sun rose over his shoulder. It rose over cities that had not been there then, and over plains that had been forests. It rose, as usual, warming the living.

2

In Kupiansk the steam engines screeched on the rails, and the sun above the brick water tank, pockmarked by shells, shone through the smoke and ashes. The front had moved so far from these parts that gunfire was no longer audible. But Soviet bombers flew west, shaking and deafening everything on the earth by their roar. And so the steam burst out noiselessly from the train whistle, and the railroad cars moved noiselessly down the tracks. And afterward, no matter how hard Tretyakov listened, he couldn't hear the sound of bombing.

The days he spent traveling from school to his house, and from home across the entire country, had blended together, the way the steel threads of the tracks endlessly streaming toward him had blended together. And now, sitting on the rusty gravel of the tracks at a dead end, his greatcoat with its lieutenant's shoulderboards under him, he ate his lunch. The wind ruffled his hair. Ever since his curly hair had been clipped in December 1941 and had fallen to the floor with all the other curly hair—dark, pitch black, red, flaxen, soft, wiry—it had never grown back. It was only on a tiny passport photo that his mother had saved that his hair survived in its prewar glory. Now it was starting to grow back.

The bumping metal buffers of the railroad cars clanged. Steam hissed. The air smelled suffocatingly of burned coal. People ran around, rushing off somewhere, jumping over the tracks: Tretyakov seemed to be the only person at the station who wasn't in a hurry.

He had stood in line for food twice today. The first time he reached the window, pushed his papers through, only to find out that he had to pay, too. He had unlearned how to buy things during the war, and he had no money on him. At the front they give you everything you're entitled to, or things simply lie about, abandoned during an attack or during a retreat, and you take as much as you can carry.

So Tretyakov had to go behind the water tank and take out the towel issued back at the military school. He hadn't even unrolled it before several people flocked around to buy the rag. They were all men of draft age who had avoided the war, and they were jumpy and fast; they tried to tear the towel out of his hands and kept looking around, ready to vanish in an instant. Disdainfully, without bargaining, he sold it for half its worth and got back in line.

The line moved slowly toward the window. Lieutenants, captains, senior lieutenants, some wearing neat new uniforms, others coming back from hospitals and wearing used uniforms, washed and mended where the bullet or shell fragment had damaged them. That whole long line on its way to the front passed by that food window. Everyone bowed his head before it: some grimly, others with an inexplicable pleading smile.

"Next!" came the voice from inside.

Submitting to a vague curiosity, Tretyakov also bowed his head and peeked into the window. Amid the sacks, open crates, and parcels, amid all that largesse, two pairs of patent leather boots stamped the groaning planks. Slightly dusty, taut at the calves, the boots had thin leather soles—they weren't for mud, they were for walking on planks.

The rearguard soldier's swift hands, the golden hairs on them sprinkled with flour, grabbed Tretyakov's food ration card and money from his fingers and put everything out on

6

the counter at once: a tin can of fish, sugar, bread, fatback, and half a pack of light tobacco.

"Next!"

A woman walked behind him, crunching the gravel, and stopped nearby.

"Treat me to a smoke, Lieutenant!"

She said it challengingly, but her eyes were hungry and shining. It's easier for a hungry person to ask for a drink or a smoke.

"Sit down," he said simply, then laughed at himself. He had just been about to tie up his pack. He hadn't cut himself another slice of bread because he wanted it to last until he got to the front, where the law is: Don't eat until you're full, eat until it's gone.

She sat down with him on the rusty rail, pulled the hem of her skirt over her thin knees, and tried not to watch him cut bread and fatback for her. Everything she wore was a hand-me-down: a soldier's shirt without a collar, a civilian skirt pinned at the side, and dried and cracked German boots with flattened, rolled-up toes. She turned away when she ate, and he saw how her back and shoulder blades shook when she swallowed a piece. He cut some more bread and fatback. She gave him a questioning glance. He understood the question and blushed: His windburned cheeks, constantly tanned for the last three years, turned brown. A knowing smile crinkled the corners of her thin lips. Her dark hand brazenly took the bread and held it with greasy fingers.

A skinny dog with chunks of fur missing on its ribs crawled out from beneath a railroad car and stared at them from a distance, whining and drooling. The woman bent down for a stone, and the dog scurried off with a squeal, its tail between its legs. A growing metal din passed through a train as the cars shuddered and rolled off down the track. Militiamen, police in blue uniforms, ran toward the train, leaped up onto the running boards, and flung themselves over the tall walls into the coal carriers.

"Cops," the woman said. "Off to pick up people." She gave him an appraising look: "From the school?"

"Yes."

"Your hair is growing in blond. But your eyebrows are so dark. . . . Is this your first time at the front?"

He chuckled. "My last!"

"Don't make jokes like that! I had a brother in the partisans . . ."

She began telling him about her brother, how he had been a commander at first, how he got out of an ambush and made it home and then joined the partisans, and how he died. She told it casually, obviously not for the first time. Maybe she was even lying; he'd heard many stories like it.

A locomotive stopped nearby to refill with water; the stream of water as thick as a column cascaded from the iron spout and everything hissed.

"I was a partisan courier too!" she shouted. Tretyakov nodded. "But you can't prove anything now!"

The steam came out of a small pipe at the end of the spout and banged on a metal sheet. They couldn't hear each other speak.

"Let's get a drink?" she shouted in his ear.

"Where?"

"There's a hydrant!"

He picked up his pack. "Let's go!"

"And then we'll have a smoke, right?" She hurried after him, hoping for the best.

When they got to the hydrant, he realized he had forgotten his coat. She offered to get it and quickly ran off in her short boots, jumping over the rails.

Would she bring it? He was ashamed to run after her.

She brought it. She came back, proudly carrying his coat and wearing his cap like a rooster comb on her head. They took turns drinking water, and laughed, and splashed each

8

other. He watched her drink, squinting her eyes, putting her mouth around the icy stream. Her hair sparkled with water mist, and in the sun her eyes were reddish brown with gold flecks. To his surprise he realized that she was his age.

She washed her boots under the stream of water—and kept glancing at him. The boots shone. She brushed off the splashes of water from her skirt. She walked with him across the entire station. They walked next to each other. He had his pack over his shoulder; she carried his coat, as if she were his sister seeing him off. Or his girlfriend. They started saying good-bye when they discovered they both were going in the same direction.

He stopped a military truck on the highway and helped her into the back. The road vanished behind them and soon they were covered with limy dust. Tretyakov spread out his coat behind their backs. Protected from the wind under the coat, they kissed like crazy.

"Stay!" she said.

The road was bumpy and they bumped teeth.

"For a day . . ."

And they knew that they would never have anything more, never. That's why they couldn't let go of each other.

They passed a platoon of women soldiers. Row after row appeared, only to be left behind by the truck and lost in a cloud of lime dust.

At the entrance to the next village she jumped down and, with a farewell wave, disappeared forever. Her last words were "Don't lose your coat!"

Soon after, the truck turned at a fork in the road and he got off too. He sat on the side of the road, smoking, waiting for a passing car, and regretting that he hadn't stayed. He hadn't even asked her name. But what was a name?

The platoon of girls marched up through the dust.

"Ha-alt!" The sergeant brought them to a stop sharply.

They stamped their feet out of rhythm. Their skin was coppery from the sun, their hair filled with dust.

"Left face!"

Straining his calf muscles, the sergeant backed up and barked, "Atten-hut!"

There were deep circles of sweat under the girls' arms. Across the road a grove of trees scattered leaves in the wind. One bulging eye squinting, the sergeant walked up and down the ranks.

"Dis-missed! To . . ." and he used an earthy term to explain what they could use the break to do.

Laughing, the girls ran across the road, pulling their carbines over their heads as they went. The sergeant, pleased with himself, came over, saluted, and sat down next to Tretyakov: bosses together. A rivulet of sweat ran down his brown temple from his cap to his cheek, leaving a shiny path.

"I'm training communications operators!" And he winked, his eye bloodshot from the wind and sun. "Can't imagine a tougher job."

They rolled cigarettes. Voices called out in the grove across the road. Gradually the platoon regrouped. The girls came back with their rifles over their shoulders. Some had a flower in their hands, others a bouquet of autumn leaves. They lined up. The sergeant barked another order.

"Let's have a song!"

A burst of laughter came in response. The sergeant just waved his hand as if to say: See, what can I do with them?

Sitting on the side of the road, waiting for a lift, Tretyakov watched the platoon of girls tramp merrily through the dust and out of sight.

3

The closer you get to the front, the more visible are the traces of an enormous slaughter. The funeral teams had come by, burying the dead; the salvage teams had come by, gathering everything that could still be used in combat; the local inhabitants had lugged home whatever the war, which had roared over them, had left behind and could be used by the living. Smashed, burned equipment rusted in the fields, and high above everything, above the stillness of death, was the prickly clarity and blueness of the autumn sky.

Along the road the infantry moved, metal lifts clicking, tin bowls rattling, the skirts of their greatcoats lashing their legs. Soldiers of all sizes and ages were marching to replace the ones who fell here. And the youngest, those who had not seen anything yet, craned their necks with the painful curiosity and shyness of the living to look at the eternal mystery of death on the field of the recent battle. Over there, where they were headed in the light of the sunset, boilers seemed to be blowing up. The air shuddered.

Tretyakov too looked around and worried—embarrassed that his thoughts were those of a first-timer. He hadn't been at the front in eight months. He had forgotten. He had to get used to it again.

He had spent last night with a stranger he had met on the outskirts of a large village the Germans had burned down.

"Senior Lieutenant Taranov!" the stranger had introduced

himself, saluting smartly and jerking his hand away from the patent leather visor as if it had been burned.

He looked like regular army. His clothes were made to fit: the greenish field shirt, the blue jodhpurs, the boots recut to resemble fancy ones. He carried a coat like those worn by officers. Even hanging on his arm the coat kept its style: The back was padded, the front puffed out, the shoulderboards lay smoothly, and the slit was perfect. A coat like that is good on parade, on horseback, but you can't use it as a blanket: whichever way you pull it on, the wind gets in. But with it, in the third year of the war, Senior Lieutenant Taranov was making his way from a reserve regiment to the front.

"You can understand how I've been itching to be part of this all this time," he said, looking into Tretyakov's eyes and shaking his hand with feeling.

Taranov had chosen the house for their overnight stay, and he had been lucky. The woman of the house, a forty-year-old Ukrainian, was happy to see officers; that meant that her house wouldn't be filled with a crowd of soldiers. And in a short while Taranov, with a towel tied around his middle, was opening cans and helping her make dinner in the kitchen. Behind her, attracted by the smell of food, was a boy of three or so, stretching to see what was on the table.

"You be off to sleep, my little misery!" the woman yelled at him, and pretending to be angry, handed him a piece of American sausage stuffing from the table.

Tretyakov went down the road to the trucks and filled the empty kerosene lamp with gasoline. He added a pinch of salt to keep the gasoline from exploding when lit. When he returned there were three people at the table.

"Just look, Lieutenant, who our hostess has been hiding from us!" Taranov cried, flashing the gold crowns on his teeth. And he winked and nodded his head in the third person's direction.

Sitting next to the hostess was her seventeen-year-old

daughter. She was good-looking, but she sat shyly, like a nun, with her black lashes lowered. When Tretyakov sat down next to her, she looked at him with curiosity. Her eyes were bright blue. She spoke first.

"We won't be blown up?"

"Of course not!" Tretyakov tried to calm her. "Add salt to gasoline and it'll never blow up."

She was smiling embarrassedly. "I'm such a coward, afraid of everything. . . ."

The mother guarded her daughter with talk, showering the table with words like bullets from a machine gun.

"The Germans came in, and I was lying in bed after surgery, all cut up. Oh, my God! Oxana was only fourteen, and the little one just born. . . . Why should I be afraid?"

"Your name is Oxana?" Tretyakov asked softly.

"Oxana. And you?"

"Volodya."

She gave him her hand—soft, hot, damp—under the table. His heart skipped a beat and started thumping.

"Oxana!" the mother called, getting up from the table. Oxana sighed, smiled at the lieutenant, and reluctantly followed her mother.

They could hear the woman's quiet voice in the other room: She was speaking quickly, but they couldn't make out a single word. "Don't be shy, Lieutenant!" Taranov whispered. "We're off to the front."

He winked and poured vodka into their glasses. They drank, and lit their cigarettes from the lamp.

"This may be your last day like this; you might get killed tomorrow, right?" Then he called loudly, "Katerina Vasilyevna! Katya! Why have you abandoned us? It's not nice. We could take offense, you know."

The voices in the other room stopped. Then the mother came out alone, with a brilliant smile.

"Where's Oxana?" Taranov asked.

"She went to sleep." She sat down next to him, her plump

shoulder caressing his. "Now if only you were doctors . . ."

"What's the matter? Who's sick?" Taranov asked.

"No one's sick. But they send us to build roads, and if you were doctors you could write a medical excuse for the girl."

"Well, we are doctors!" Taranov kept winking at Tretyakov, nodding his head toward the door that led to Oxana.

"Oh, you're just joking!" She waggled her plump hand at him. "Doctors' shoulderboards are completely different!"

"What kind of shoulderboards do doctors have?"

"Teeny-tiny." And with her other hand she traced the size on his shoulderboard. "Teeny-tiny . . ."

"You're sure they're not biggie-wiggie?" Taranov's gold crowns glistened, and a cold sore showed on the inside of his lower lip. "Not biggie-wiggie?"

The conversation was all in their eyes now. Tretyakov got up and said he was going for a smoke. He found his coat and his pack in the dark hallway. Shutting the front door, he could hear Taranov's muffled voice and the woman's laughter.

Leaning against the one remaining post of the fence, he stood in the yard and smoked. He felt lousy. The woman was protecting her daughter, of course. Maybe she had done the same thing with the Germans, distracting them from the girl.

Silently, the western sky shuddered with artillery flashes. The rain-washed crescent of the new moon, filled to the brim with blue light, hung over the fire, and the clumsy shadow of a burned tree sprawled in the yard. The acrid smell of smoke came from the next house. Charred apple trees, once planted beneath the windows, surrounded a collapsed chimney in a pile of ashes.

He could hear the drivers chatting near their trucks across the way. Tretyakov went over to them. People were sleeping on the floor of the house. He went up a rickety ladder to the hayloft, piled up some dusty-smelling hay in the dark, lay down, and pulled his coat up over his head. As he fell asleep, he heard the drivers talking downstairs and the slow hum of a plane high above the roof.

The next morning he met Senior Lieutenant Taranov at the headquarters of the artillery brigade. He had walked about six kilometers at dawn and had arrived early. The clerks were just sitting down at their desks. They didn't feel like taking on any duties until their superiors came, so they looked busy by opening file drawers and slamming them shut.

The regiments of the artillery brigade were scattered across the wide front, but the headquarters was in a farm four kilometers from the front line. Every so often distant artillery explosions shook up the quiet and the indolence of the farmhouse, and when the wind shifted, the sound of machine guns reached them. But the wasp buzzing on the windowpane was louder.

Smoke from the summer-house kitchen blew in from the yard. A woman was doing the wash in a wooden trough under the cherry trees. A mountain of pants and shirts lay on the grass, and a kettle of underwear was boiling on the campfire. Clerk Ferisov, young but already balding, had volunteered to help her. He broke a branch, tossed it into the fire, and stirred the kettle—all the time keeping his eyes on the woman's breasts, swaying heavily in the opening of her shirt, or on her arms, bare to the shoulder, moving in the suds. The other men called out advice through the window. Only Senior Clerk Kalistratov was getting ready for work; he was cleaning out his cigarette holder by pulling a straw through it. When he pulled it out it was covered with wet brown muck from the nicotine. He sniffed it with disgust and shook his head.

The clerk at the window squashed the wasp. Pleased, he wiped his fingers on the wall, took an apple from his pocket, and bit in with a crunch. White juice foamed on his teeth.

"So what kind of a watch did the scout bring you, Semioshkin?" Kalistratov asked as he carefully pulled a fresh straw through the cigarette holder.

Semioshkin squirmed on the windowsill and said, "A Dox!"

"They get all the breaks, those scouts." Kalistratov held the cigarette holder up to the light. "They go first and get all the best stuff."

The clerks paid no attention to Tretyakov. Lots of lieutenants like him passed through headquarters on their way from school to the front. Some of them didn't even have time to wear out their uniforms when the news came back in the opposite direction, crossing them off the lists, stopping all further supplies, which they wouldn't need anymore.

Before breakfast the intelligence brigade chief dropped by. The clerks leaped to attention. Papers appeared magically on their desks. A bespectacled clerk who had not been there at all before materialized at the typewriter in the corner. He must have been hiding under the desk.

The intelligence chief took an instant liking to Tretyakov. "Kalistratov, tell them I'm keeping the lieutenant! He'll stay here with me, be a platoon commander." Instead of being pleased, instead of feeling grateful, Tretyakov requested to be sent to the front. From that moment on, the clerks made a point of not noticing him.

Tretyakov went outside to wait for the messenger from the regiment. The woman took the kettle from the fire and dumped the pile of boiled underwear and soapy water into the trough, a cloud of steam hitting her in the face. Sitting on a pile of shirts, his bare feet sticking out, was a two-year-old boy, holding a tomato in both fists, sucking its juice. His shirt was stained with seeds and tomato juice. "He must have been born fatherless," Tretyakov thought lazily. He had gotten up early this morning, and the morning sun made him sleepy. The tops of his boots were dusty. He was thinking about cleaning them with grass when he saw the messenger.

The soldier walked quickly with a rolling gait, looking up occasionally at the wires that led to headquarters. Tretyakov waited a bit and then followed him inside. The messenger had handed over his message and was drinking water by the door.

The senior clerk held the message far from his eyes and read it with a severe look on his face, while the messenger leaned his rifle against the wall and rolled himself a smoke.

"From Three-sixteen?" Tretyakov asked.

The messenger licked the edge of the piece of newspaper to hold his tobacco, lit up, took a long drag, and asked, squinting in the smoke, "Are you the one I am to accompany, Comrade Lieutenant?"

His sun-bleached eyebrows were white with dust and his scratched face looked whitewashed. After several drags on the cigarette, the messenger, enveloped in smoke, suddenly remembered something.

"How could I forget? . . . I'm getting old." He got up and unbuttoned the pocket of his shirt. He took out a rag, gray with dust, and unwrapped it in the palm of his hand. It held a silver medal, *For Valor.*

The clerks gathered round, read the accompanying congratulations, and examined the medal. It was struck in the old style, with a red ribbon on a small peg. The silver was tarnished, as if covered by soot, and there was an indentation and hole in the middle. A bullet had gone through the soft metal, and the number on the back was illegible.

"Which Suntsov was this?" Kalistratov asked, clearly proud of his ability to know the men by name. "The one who joined us at Gulkevichi with the reserve troops?"

"I don't know," the messenger said, smiling kindly and wiping his neck and face with his cap again. "My orders were to bring it to headquarters and give it back."

17

"So how did he die?"

"How? Sniper probably. He was a scout."

"Radio man. It says: *Communications*."

"Was he? Well then, in communications," the soldier said. "Killed while maintaining communications . . ."

The senior clerk looked grim. He took the medal and added the appropriate document. And as he opened the metal box with its creaking lid, he was solemn and severe, performing a rite. The silver medal hit the metal bottom with a ringing sound, and the lid went back down with a creak.

Soon after, Tretyakov followed the messenger out and headed for the regiment. They turned down an alley, and toward them, along its entire width—from wattle fence to wattle fence—came a group of officers returning from breakfast.

A major was telling a story while an officer on the far right looked across the entire line of men, smilingly participating in the conversation. To his surprise, Tretyakov recognized him as Senior Lieutenant Taranov, his gold tooth shining between his flabby lips. But in his manner and deportment he belonged with this group of officers, as if he had always been there.

4

That evening, while Tretyakov was helping to bring guns to the front, Captain Povysenko, commander of the battery, ran over to him in the twilight and pointed his fingernail at the map.

"See that little ravine? See the hill? You'll set up the guns on the other side of the slope." The fingernail, black with nicotine stains, made a line. "Is that clear? My observation point will be on hill One thirty-two. You'll set up the battery and put in a line to me." Then he repeated, "Is that clear?"

"It's clear," Tretyakov said. On the map everything was clear.

A tractor was running nearby. Sparks, brilliant in the twilight, showered from its exhaust pipe. The guns, sheathed in tarps and in traveling position, had been mounted already. A sergeant was busy near the trailer that carried the battery's equipment. Captain Povysenko's steady gaze moved in that direction and he went over.

In the trailer, under the tarpaulin top, Commander Zavgorodny of the gun platoon was on his hands and knees, doubled up with pain. They had wanted to send him to a hospital unit, but at the front a sick man somehow feels like a malingerer. Here you either get wounded or you get killed. Now you're alive, in an hour you're dead—does it matter whether you were killed in good health or not? A sergeant had mixed up a half glass of kerosene and salt and made

Zavgorodny drink it. "First it burns, and then you feel relief. . . ."

Povysenko came around the back and looked into the trailer.

"Well, do you feel better?"

The sergeant looked in too. "Is it still burning? Is it?" He felt responsible—both for the "cure" and the illness.

"It's getting better," Zavgorodny groaned. His knees moved on the coats; he was unable to lie down.

"It's a tried-and-true method," the sergeant encouraged him. "First it burns, and then you feel relief. . . ." He rubbed his chest, down to the strap buckle, where the relief would come.

The low sky was oppressive, and there was a pre-rain stillness in the air. The tractors with the guns on their trailers were ready; to the right, beyond the cornfields, machine guns sounded, and tracer bullets flew up above the earth, bright and clear.

"So, this is it." The battery commander thought a bit, chewing his chapped lips. "I'm taking your platoon with me. Paravyan, the assistant to the platoon commander, will be with you, just in case. Is everything clear? Then go!"

He saluted and his raincoat rustled as he moved away.

With a grumble, the tractors pulled the guns, squashing bushes and young trees in their path. A deep, churned-up path was left in the soil by the battery's progress.

They traveled without lights. Above them was the black sky, underfoot and ahead lay the dusty road. It began to rain. Thick black mud attached itself to the heavy wheels of the cannons, to the rubber tires.

The front was always to their right. Rockets flew up and went out, extinguished by the rain. In the vague unsteady reflections of each rocket Tretyakov saw soldiers in wet raincoats slogging behind the guns. And on each cannon several people huddled, sleeping, while the rain poured down.

"Paravyan! Chase them off the guns! If we get hit from above, they'll be hurt."

Paravyan, a handsome and graceful man, looked at him. He silently disapproved, but went to obey the order.

"Do you want those men to be squashed? How many times do I have to tell you!?"

Tretyakov knew that he'd have to keep telling him for as long as they traveled. He had been a foot soldier and been chased off like that. But as soon as his commander was looking in the other direction, he would climb back up on the gun because he was sleepy, and it was better to sleep sitting down than marching. But now it wasn't someone else who was responsible for him, and whom he could curse under his breath. He was in command of these men and was responsible for them; that's why he gave the order to chase them off.

He didn't know any of them, except for Paravyan, not by face or by name. He led them; they followed him. He hadn't had time to meet any of the men in his own platoon either. When he was brought to headquarters that morning, Chabarov, who was substituting for the killed platoon commander, was ordered to hand over command to Lieutenant Tretyakov. Chabarov, an old front-line soldier, took a look at the nineteen-year-old lieutenant, said nothing, and took Tretyakov to meet his men.

The entire platoon, all the men who weren't at their observation posts, were digging bomb shelters behind the hut— not for themselves, but for the headquarters staff.

In the sun the soldiers' bodies, even after an entire summer, were white. Only their faces, necks, and hands were tanned. They were young men, just coming into manly strength; they had shaped up during the war. Only two or three men were older, wiry, with muscles stretched by work and skin that was beginning to sag. One stood out; as powerful as a wrestler, his chest covered with a mat of black hair from neck to waist. When he raised his pick, it wasn't his ribs but his muscles that showed beneath his skin.

As Tretyakov looked over those sweaty glistening bodies, he saw many old wounds, covered with scar tissue, and he saw himself through the eyes of these men. Before these hard-working men, stripped to the waist, stood a young officer, fresh out of school, in a neat cap, all new, like a shell out of its case. Chabarov had a reason for introducing him to the platoon that way. He had picked that moment. Tretyakov couldn't start explaining that he had seen combat, that he had been at the front.

Later, when it was time to go to lunch, Chabarov had the platoon line up, with their rifles and bowls in their hands, and turned over the list he had written himself. Chabarov made it clear that he respected discipline but was waiting to see if he would respect the new platoon commander. The platoon stood there, looking at Tretyakov, and at the piece of paper on which Chabarov had written their names.

"Dzhedzhelashvili!" called Tretyakov. He wondered why two "dzhe's" were necessary, when one was plenty. He had decided that the Georgian name went with the big soldier covered with black chest hair.

"Present!"

A young boy took a step forward. He was blond with a carrot-colored blush on his cheek, reddish-brown eyes, and a merry gaze: Dzhedzhelashvili. The big black soldier turned out to be Nasrullaev. And no matter whose name he called, it never seemed to fit the face. And for the time being, it was this way for him: The list one thing, the platoon another.

Tretyakov no longer had a good idea of where he was. By three hundred hours the guns had to be in firing position, and they hadn't even passed the Yasenevka farmstead. "You'll see the Yasenevka farm," the commander had said, trying to make out the name in the worn crease of the map. "You'll see for yourself. . . . Bear right there and keep right. . . ." But they had been on the road one hour, then two, and no matter how hard Tretyakov peered in the glare of the rockets that went up over the wet road, no farmstead was visible. Horrified by the thought that he was leading them in the wrong direction, terrified of the shame, he did the only thing he could; the less confidence there was in him, the more confidently he went.

At last something dark loomed ahead of them. A rocket went up and Tretyakov had time to make out long, low sheds and something taller above them. Must be poplars. Then the rocket went out and they were plunged into total darkness again.

He hurried, overjoyed, his boots slipping in the soggy black earth, to pass the front tractor, and waved his hand: Follow me.

What he had taken at a distance for sheds turned out to be a battery of 122-mm guns. Tied up like wagons, the long-barreled guns and tractors stood by the side of the road, one behind the other. Then someone was coming toward him.

"Turn off your engines!"

"Why?"

"Can't you see what's up ahead?"

Seeing nothing and understanding only that it wasn't the farmstead, which meant they had made a wrong turn, Tretyakov asked, "Yasenevka is supposed to be around here. Yasenevka . . . Is it far?"

The man's face, which he could barely make out under the rain hood, seemed old and wrinkled.

"About five kilometers to the farm."

"What do you mean, five? It was four, and we've been traveling two hours already."

"Well, maybe it's four kilometers." The man waved his hand indifferently. "You're the platoon leader? I'm one too. You got one-fifty-two howitzers? So do I, the same devils. Fifteen tons with the tractor! And the bridge ahead you can knock over with your shoulder."

23

They went over to look at the bridge. Soldiers from both batteries followed them. They reached the middle of the slippery wet logs. Below there was a ravine or a dried river-bed—too dark to tell.

"And Yasenevka is on the other side?"

"Why are you harping on that Yasenevka? Yasenevka, Yasenevka . . . Do you have that bridge on your map? Neither do I." The leader opened his map case and flicked his fingernail against the celluloid covering the barely visible map. He wiped the rain from the map with his sleeve. "It's not on the map, but there it is!" And to make his point more strongly, he kicked the logs with his heel. He even jumped up and down. Soldiers from both batteries stood around them. And 'if it's not on the map, then it shouldn't be here on the ground. Or since it is here, then put it on the map. That's the way I see it."

The way he really saw it, since they didn't put it on the map, he didn't have to deal with it.

So Tretyakov had to run down the slope, getting his knees wet in the tall grass, and go beneath the bridge. The supports were big logs held by brackets from above. When he looked at the whole thing from below, it seemed quite undependable.

They had been taught in school how to calculate the maximum load for bridges, but only the devil could figure it out now, when you couldn't see a thing, and the other platoon leader's voice was buzzing in his ears. The man was right behind him, banging his fist on every support.

"Look at that! Look at that! They won't be able to hold that weight." He tried digging with his finger. "And it's all rotten, too." Convincing Tretyakov of this seemed more important to him than the war itself.

A rocket flared up and the ravine was filled with murky light. The bridge appeared above it: the plank cover, the people in the rain. A truck carcass lay among the rocks; rain lashed the wet roof, crumpled like a tin can. "Why is he so determined to convince me?" Tretyakov thought angrily. Hating the man for his own uncertainty, he climbed up.

He approached the first gun.

"Who are the drivers?"

The soldiers looked from one to another; then one man, standing nearby and looking around harder than the rest, said, "Me," as if he had just found himself among the others. But he did not come forward. He remained with the rest. He felt more secure that way.

"Gun commanders and drivers, come here!" Tretyakov ordered, separating them from the battery.

One man after another came forward, until there were six. The tractor drivers were easy to identify: They were covered with soot.

"Get all the men away from the guns. Gun commander, you'll go first. Each man in front of his gun. Drivers, you'll drive in first gear. When one gets over, the next one drives. Is that clear?"

Silence.

"Am I speaking clearly?"

They responded hesitantly, unevenly: "Clear. . . ." Behind them the battery stood in silence. They were together, and he, who had been put in charge, unknown to them and known for nothing, was alone. It wasn't that they didn't trust the bridge; they didn't trust him.

"Is that your tractor?" Pointing, Tretyakov asked the driver who had been looking around most.

"That one?" The driver was playing for time. The exhaust pipe on the tractor was raspberry red at the base and raindrops turned to steam as they hit it. "It's mine."

"Name?"

"What's the difference, Comrade Lieutenant? My name's Semakin."

"You, Semakin, will drive the first gun."

"I will, Comrade Lieutenant!" Semakin spoke loudly and waved his arm recklessly. "I'll drive. I always obey orders!"

He was shaking his head negatively as he spoke. "But how will we tow the tractor from there? It'll end up under the bridge, and so will the gun. . . ."

"I will stand under the bridge if you're scared, afraid to drive over the bridge. You'll drive the gun over me!" He gave orders: "Drivers, take your places, soldiers, get over by the guns!" And he led the battery to the bridge.

When the treads of the tractor rested on the first log planks, Tretyakov ran below.

"Go!" He waved his arm and shouted, even though they couldn't hear him up above. And he went to meet his fate beneath the bridge.

Everything overhead was sagging and creaking, the weight rolling from log to log. The supports seemed to be sinking. Then the cannon rolled onto the bridge. The bridge groaned and shifted. "It'll collapse!" He held his breath. The logs rubbed against each other, stuff fell down on him. His eyes were filled with dust; he was blinded and rubbed them with his callused fingers, trying to make out what was happening above him. It was impossible. Above the engine's backfiring he could hear wood creaking.

Without seeing it, he sensed the enormous weight drive off the bridge onto solid ground. The bridge sighed above him. Only then did he realize how much power had pushed down from above; his tense muscles felt as if he himself had been holding up the bridge with his back.

Tretyakov came out of the ravine; he wasn't going to stand under the bridge the whole time. This wasn't the circus, after all. It would have been much simpler just to have gotten into the tractor with the driver and calmly led the battery across. It would have been less noisy and more useful.

By the middle of the night, they had reached the farm and had awoken an old man to show them the local roads. He sat in the tractor in nothing but his underwear, probably hoping that they would feel sorry for him and let him go home sooner. Instead, they gave him a quilted jacket, and he huddled in it, rubbing one foot with the other.

"Here, here . . . down this way . . ." His skinny chicken neck with clumps of white fuzz stuck out from the collar.

"Here, here," the driver mocked him. "Where are you leading me? Women go to piss here. Take me where a gun can pass!"

The old man blinked his tearing eyes obediently, and his trembling hand pointed straight ahead, into the rain. He led the battery to a stand of trees and they let him go.

They turned off the engines. A machine gun fired nearby. Traces of the bullets glimmered from the blackness of the earth, appearing and disappearing. The front was not far, and Tretyakov was stuck here with his heavy guns.

The drivers approached him:

"Out of fuel, Comrade Lieutenant."

"What do you mean?"

"Used it up. We've been driving all night."

"How can you be out of fuel?" Tretyakov asked.

They stood before him, looking at the ground and saying nothing. They could stand like that forever, he saw that. Not knowing what to do now or what to say, Tretyakov walked away. He thought he heard Zavgorodny calling him from the trailer, he heard a groan; but he pretended not to hear. He didn't need consolation. Anyway, what could the sick man do from in there.

There were horses wandering around in the stand of trees. One pale horse was squinting and nibbling on tree bark. Steam rose from the mare's neck. Tretyakov noticed that the rain had stopped. Fog was rising from the earth, from the grass.

He heard voices and moved closer. Panting and swearing under their breath, a crew was rolling a gun into a freshly dug foxhole. These were the positions for the divisional cannon. Tretyakov located the platoon commander, an elderly-looking man wearing infantry leg wrappings and boots, each holding a pound or so of soil. The commander listened suspiciously to Tretyakov at first. At last he understood. They compared maps, and suddenly it was all clear. The slope where Tretyakov was supposed to position his guns was just half a kilometer away.

Hurrying to finish before daylight, Tretyakov found the battery's positions, checked everything, figured out which road to take, and returned to the trees. The soldiers were sleeping, and only Paravyan, wrapped in his rain cape, patrolled near the guns. He gave orders for everyone to get up. Cold in their damp jackets and having found no warmth in sleep, the drivers came over, shivering and yawning. When Tretyakov explained where he was taking the guns, fuel was suddenly found.

"There was a little in those canisters," they said, averting their eyes.

Well, the drivers had been right in their own way; driving around all night with no goal in sight really would have used up all the fuel.

Before dawn, when the damp dark grew darker, Tretyakov left the men to dig foxholes for the guns and run the wires to the observation point.

Chabarov was setting up a stereo receiver in a new foxhole.

"Where's the battery commander?"

"He's sleeping up there."

A rocket flared up in the front line, and Tretyakov saw him, his rain cape over his head, his wet boots sticking out, sleeping behind the parapet.

"Comrade Captain! Comrade Captain!"

Povysenko sat up, squinting in the rocket's glare. He looked around, not totally awake.

"What took you so long? What's your name again, Chetverikov?"

"Tretyakov."

"Right, Tretyakov, I remember. You're slower than mo-lasses."

He stood up, stretched, yawned and moaned, and woke up.

"Have the foxholes been dug yet?"

"They're digging."

Tretyakov still had the roar of the tractors in his ears, and his legs still seemed to be slogging through mud. But after the sleepless night his head was light and clear, and the huge battery commander in his rain cape kept looming very close and then receding in the reddish glare.

5

For several days battles took place in that region. The unharvested wheat field between the German and Russian foxholes was covered with rubble from the explosions and pitted with black holes. During the night, scouts crawled through the wheat: Russians toward the Germans, Germans toward the Russians. And suddenly great bursts of gunfire would begin, and someone would be dragged along the trenches, one of the war's nameless victims, the heels of his boots and the yellowed fingers of his dangling hand making marks in the dirt.

One hot day the wheat field went up in flames from a shot. A whirlwind came up, fanned the flames, and blew them across the foxholes and along the front lines and on to the hill where Tretyakov sat at the observation point. There was nothing left but grass burned down to the roots, dust and ashes. The oily smell of burned grain was in everything: the air, the food, the clothes.

Tretyakov looked at his hands, the soot eating into his skin, thick and black around his broken nails, and remembered how clean they were in 1942 at the swamp near Staraya Russa, when his skin was wrinkled and soggy, as if he had been doing laundry. They had spent so much time in the middle of the swamp on a tiny island between the Russians' lines and the Germans'. They never lit a fire, and everything they wore was damp. The spring was late that year, and cold. It suddenly snowed in early May, a wind-driven blizzard dropping large snowflakes even as the sun shone, making the grass that poked out from beneath the snow even greener.

And he would never forget how he jumped up in the middle of the night, hearing the whispered word "Germans!" Shivering, his teeth chattering, afraid at seventeen years he would be taken for a coward, Tretyakov peered over the parapet and could make out nothing. The tension and cold made his eyes tear. Then, softly, a wave lashed at the bushes. Then another one came across the water, rocking the moonlight. Shadow after shadow, the white crest, from bush to bush—four of them. Only waves rising and falling.

There in the bushes they shot all four with their carbines. In the stupidity of his youth he crawled over to look at the Germans: What were they like? He wanted to clarify something in his own mind and was almost killed: One of the German scouts was still alive. Tretyakov dragged him over, and when they were bandaging him, weakening and covered with death sweat, he realized to his surprise that he had no anger, no hatred for the man, even though the German had just shot at him.

Now, sitting in this observation post, he still had not figured out many things for himself. The war was in its third year, and things that had been incomprehensible had become habitual and simple. Time passed according to its own laws during the war; things that happened a long time ago sometimes seemed near and clear, as if it were yesterday, while the longest, slowest, and most never-ending was what was happening at the moment. It seemed as if he had spent half his life sitting on the burned-out hill, in that usual front-line state: not asleep, not awake—ready at any moment to go to sleep or to leap up into battle.

Just when they had gotten used to the place, and could tell by the sound which German battery was shooting from where, the orders came to wrap up their telephones and quickly return to fire positions. They took down the rain cape that served as an entrance to their dugout and hurriedly crumbled the straw on their plank beds.

Under the high moon they crawled along the burned terrain, rolling up the wire. The Germans were shooting nervously, sending up rocket after rocket. When you were spread out, fully visible on bare ground, the shooting seemed closer. Every rocket seemed to hang directly over you. That was when you remembered how good it was sitting in the dugout, how safe.

Once they were over the hill, in the valley, they walked. Here the grass was tall, covered with dew, and Tretyakov washed his hands in it and laughed out loud. He had gotten so used to the smell of burned grain that he had stopped noticing it, but here, in the fresh air, he realized that he had been smoked through.

Carrying the spools of wire, shovels, and earphones, plus all their belongings and weapons, they caught up with the battery on the march. In a cloud of dust raised by feet and wheels, the infantry moved along the front. When the units were in the trenches, the dugouts, and the foxholes, it didn't look like there was anyone around to fight. But when the troops piled out on the road, and the front of the column and its end were lost in dust, Russia looked as if it had many men.

Dawn found them in the woods. Somewhere behind them the guns were still dragging along, but Tretyakov's platoon, which had traveled ahead in the night, was sleeping on the ground. The woods smelled of autumn, of a campfire. A soldier was stirring a sooty bucket over the fire. In the week that he had been with the regiment, Tretyakov had not yet learned the names of all the men in his platoon, but he recognized this soldier. The flat face glistening with oil, the squinting eyes. Kytin! The name just jumped out at him: Kytin!

Flames licked the greasy, smoking bucket. Kytin had a

taste, looked doubtful, thought, added salt, and stirred it in. That made the meaty steam pour out harder, and Tretyakov felt hungry.

"What are you cooking there, Kytin?"

The soldier turned around. "Awake, Comrade Lieutenant?"

"I said, what are you cooking there?"

"It was running around here on four legs . . . with horns."

"How did it talk?"

Kytin's eyes narrowed to slits. "Ba-ah!" he bleated. "Bring your foot cloths over to the fire, Comrade Lieutenant, so you can get them warm."

"They dried in the sun."

He crumpled the foot cloths with his sooty fingers to soften them and put on his boots. Infantrymen, knocked out by exhaustion, slept all over the woods. Those who had fallen behind were still coming in, practically sleepwalking; seeing their own troops, they collapsed on the ground to sleep. A nurse ran from soldier to soldier, wiping away tears from her cheek.

"There was just one thermometer left and someone had to steal it!" she complained to Tretyakov. She didn't know him, but who else was there to complain to? She was around thirty, and her permanent wave was filled with dust. Who would want her thermometer? It must have broken or gotten lost, and there she was looking for it, and crying. She was exhausted. She had been on the night-long march with the rest of the troops. The soldiers were sleeping, but she was still going from man to man, waking them up, making them take off their boots, putting salves and powders on their feet. Blisters and calluses aren't bullets, but they knock you off your feet. It was women Tretyakov pitied most at war. Especially ones like her—not pretty and highstrung. Things were always harder for them—even the war.

He found a mortar hole filled with water. Young trees had

fallen around it; some of them would survive. He took off his cap and coat and got to his knees. A tuft of white cloud scudded across the mirroring surface of the water, and he saw himself in it; someone black stared up at him. The dust-filled stubble of his beard made his cheeks look dark; his sunken eyes were rimmed with black; his cheekbones were taut and chapped. In just one week he no longer looked like himself. He pushed the dry leaves that had fallen on the water to one side, along with a water bug skittering weightlessly on thin spidery legs. The water, like that in peat bogs, was brown; but when he scooped it up into his hand, it was transparent, clean, and cold. He hadn't been able to wash like that in a long time; he even pulled the straps of his undershirt from his shoulders. Then, after he dried his neck and face with the bottom of his shirt, he put the cap on his wet, combed hair and buttoned up his standing collar on his throat. He felt clean and refreshed. But he couldn't cough the dust out of his lungs—he had swallowed so much during the night!

All this time there was a howl in the sky. The Russian heavy artillery was firing mortar shells, and the explosions made leaves fall from the trees. Coming to the edge of the forest, Tretyakov jumped into a sand trench and almost stepped on the feet of a soldier lying on the bottom. He was in full uniform and fully packed and lay there as if asleep. His shaved round head was buried under the rubble of another shell that had come after the one that had killed him.

Tretyakov went around the trench. There were many fresh mortar holes in the ground—in front, behind, and direct hits on the trench—the fire had been heavy. That was the noise they had heard when they were coming.

Resting his elbows on the sandy parapet, he looked at the field in front of him. It sloped into a valley, where machine guns were firing, the roof of a cow shed shone like glass, and pyramid poplars stood like sentries before an old burial mound. The head of a sunflower, turned to the sun, was a bright-yellow splash of color.

He was using binoculars, planning how, when the sun had set behind the burial mound, he would extend communications to the infantry. Which would be the best way to lay the wires so that the shells wouldn't get him? When he left, he came across another dead soldier. He was sitting, slid all the way down. The chest of his coat was covered with fresh blood, and he didn't have any face left at all. The bloody gray chunks of brain seemed to be trembling on the sandbags of the trench.

His platoon was picnicking when he got back. An enameled basin stood in the middle and the soldiers took turns ladling from it. Chabarov, the deputy, his legs crossed tailor fashion, sat in the place of honor by the basin. Seeing the lieutenant, he banged his spoon on his bowl, and the soldiers stirred and started getting up and getting dressed.

"Go on eating," Tretyakov said.

But Chabarov looked around severely, and Kytin pulled the bowl they had left in the hot ashes and handed it to the lieutenant. They were all together, a unit, and he was still an outsider. Spreading his coat under him, Tretyakov sat down and began eating. The soup of young goat was thick and rich and the meat was sweet and juicy.

He looked at them, alive and happy in the face of death. After the meal he smoked and told Chabarov to give him two men that night—a scout and a signalman. But something else was going on in his mind. He kept seeing the sandy trench hit with shells. Did only the great not vanish forever? Were they the only ones allowed to remain among the living even after death, while the ordinary people, like all of them sitting now in this forest and the ones who had been sitting there before them, would be allowed to disappear? You live, they bury you, and then it's as if you had never existed, as if you had never lived under the sun, under this eternal blue sky where a plane was humming now, scaling unthinkable heights. Would unspoken thoughts and pain disappear without a trace? Or would something remain, floating invisibly, and when the right time came, find an echo in someone's heart? Who could divide them up into great and nongreat when they hadn't had time to live yet? Maybe the greatest—a future Pushkin or Tolstoy—were left unknown on battlefields and would never say anything to the world. Would the world feel that emptiness and loss?

6

A half hour before the start of artillery preparation Tretyakov jumped down into his foxhole. Kytin was napping, his coat collar up, the back of his head resting against the earthen wall; he opened his eyes and shut them again. Suyarov was crouching and greedily inhaling the smoke from his homegrown shag cigarette, spitting between his knees. Recognizing the lieutenant, he waved at the tobacco cloud around his head out of politeness.

"Will you have some vodka, Comrade Lieutenant?" Kytin asked.

In the pre-dawn light his flat face looked Mongolian. Yet he was from a village near Tambov. Think how far his ancestors had traveled to kill his other ancestors. And now both bloods lived peacefully within him.

"Where'd you get vodka?"

"This infantry sergeant . . ." Kytin yawned like a puppy, showing the roof of his palate. His eyes were moist; he must have truly been asleep. "In the infantry, they announce the losses the next day. First they give them vodka, then announce the losses. Do you know how much vodka they'll have tomorrow?!"

Tretyakov looked at his watch. "It's already today, not tomorrow. Come on, let's have a shot."

He drank from the cap, and the vodka seemed weak, almost like water. It just made him feel a little warmer in his

39

chest. He stood there, digging his toe into the clay of the dugout wall. They were here, the final, irreversible minutes. In the dark, breakfast was passed out to the infantrymen, and even though no one said it, they all thought as they scraped their bowls clean: This may be the last time. Did the Germans feel that too?

And in those minutes, when nothing seemed to be happening and you were just waiting, you could hear the silent movement of history. Suddenly you felt quite clearly how the whole machine, fed by the efforts of thousands and thousands of people, was moving, not through anyone's will but on its own, by its own momentum, unstoppable.

Tretyakov spent the rest of the night in the dugout of the company commander, whom he would be supporting with fire. They didn't sleep. The company commander drank tea and talked about the time he was in the hospital, in Syzrani, and what a good woman the chief doctor there had been. In the low-ceilinged dugout his eyes glowed soft and meek.

Tretyakov listened to him, spoke, but all the time had the strange feeling that this wasn't happening to him. They were sitting underground, drinking tea, waiting for the hour. And on the other side, maybe the Germans were not sleeping and waiting, too. And then, both sides would jump out of their foxholes and run to kill each other.

He had three mugs of tea and learned that this was the very regiment in which his stepfather had served. But the number had been changed because its banner had been captured in 1942, and the regiment was re-formed and re-named. His mother had had a letter from someone in this regiment: The man had seen his stepfather killed as they were breaking out of an encirclement, and he had written to her. But still hope remained—there were so many incredible mistakes in the war! And trying to trick fate, afraid to shatter the last hope, Tretyakov asked cautiously:

"I had an uncle in your regiment. Commander of Saper

40

Platoon, Junior Lieutenant Bezaits. Near Kharkov. Did you happen to know him?"

The word "uncle" had slipped out on its own, so that it wouldn't be about his stepfather if the answer were "killed."

"Bezaits . . . hm, a memorable name, you know. . . . Here's whom you should ask: Posokhin, chief of staff of the battalion, the senior adjutant. Bezaits. . . . He must remember. I wasn't near Kharkov. I joined this regiment after the hospital."

In May 1942, when the advance began near Kharkov, Tretyakov wrote his stepfather a deliriously childish letter, saying that he envied him, that he would be in the fray himself, too. . . . But by then the Germans had surrounded Kharkov.

His mother's face had trembled so pitifully when she asked him at the train station: "You'll be right there, on the southwestern front . . . in the same places. . . . Maybe you'll be able to learn something about Igor Leonidovich." She always used his stepfather's formal name when he was around, and even now she was too shy to do otherwise.

Tretyakov had felt the first stirrings for his stepfather when the war started and Bezaits was called up. The three of them—his mother, his sister Lyalya, and himself—went off to the draft board set up outside Lyalya's school. His stepfather was waiting for them, sitting right on the curb, his back against the brick column of the school gate, behaving like a stranger in a strange city, sitting right on the street, his hands on his pointy knees. He saw them coming toward him and got up, calmly brushing off his pants in the back, and embraced Tretyakov's mother. Tall and thin in a cotton shirt, a cap on his head, he pressed her face to the buttons on his chest. He stared straight ahead and caressed her hair. It seemed that he could see everything that awaited her.

Tretyakov was amazed by how skinny his stepfather's legs looked in the black foot cloths. And on those skinny legs, in his enormous soldier's boots, he went off to war. All those years that they had lived in one apartment, he had never noticed his stepfather. Now his heart ached for him.

That time when he saw his mother after military school, she seemed so much older, so flat somehow. With veins in her neck. And Lyalya had changed in two years. Unrecognizable. The war was on; there was nothing to eat—but she had blossomed. When he had left for the war, there was nothing to look at—all knees and two thin braids down her skinny back. But now when she walked down the street with him, officers turned to look at her.

Tretyakov looked at his watch and grabbed his tobacco pouch, then realized he didn't have time to roll a cigarette.

"Let me finish yours!"

He took Suyarov's cigarette, had several drags, and stood up in the foxhole. The sun had not yet risen, but he could feel the light on his face. He could feel the air over his head; bullets flew past in it—above and below, in several layers.

The three of them stood in the foxhole and looked toward the Germans. From the field of sunflowers up ahead, earth splashed up, a roar engulfed everything, and from that moment on the rumble and roar and shaking never stopped.

There was a hiss low over their heads. They bent over before they realized what was happening.

"Check the line!" Tretyakov shouted, joyfully conscious of one thing: He was alive!

There was another screech. The Germans were shooting at the battery. It was impossible to tell from where. Everything ahead of them was in smoke. The Russian planes rushed into the smoke with a roar and were visible only as black shadows. Fire flashed in front of their wings. It looked as if they were coming down low onto the field. They flew over the farm—and several explosions shot up toward them from the roofs.

The rumbling and roaring were still going on, but everyone felt the silence descend on the front units. This was the moment, this was the pull of gravity as the infantry rose into attack, tearing itself away from the ground.

"Ra-a-a-ah!" came the end of the battle cry. And then the rattle of rifles, the long *rat-a-tat* of machine guns.

The men of the infantry had burst out of the foxholes, and bent over, as if in pain, they ran across the field, hiding in the dust of the explosions, in the smoke.

When the three of them, dragging the telephone cable behind them, jumped down into the trench, the infantry was far ahead, in the sunflowers. They were amazed, as they were in every German trench; Russian artillery beat down on them, but there were almost no dead Germans. Did they carry them away with them? There was just one dead machine gunner lying next to an overturned machine gun.

The very next minute all three fell to the bottom of the trench. They lay, covering their heads with their hands, with whatever they could get hold of. Suyarov, the spool on his head, crawled to a corner. When the attack was over, Tretyakov sat up. The German machine gunner was still lying on his back in the trench, like a dummy. His glasses were dusty, but whole, not even cracked; the dead man's white nose stuck out from them.

Kytin sat up and spat—his mouth and nose were filled with dirt. The air was stifling with the smell of explosives. Smoke lay low on the ground. One at a time they crawled out of the trench. The sunflowers were still in the field, bright yellow in the smoke, their heads turned to them. Beyond, the sun rose over the battlefield.

Lying on his back, Tretyakov bent a heavy sunflower down to him. It was topheavy, filled with ripe seeds, like bullets. He broke off a section of the flower.

"Come on!"

He tossed a handful of seeds into his mouth and ran down the field, spitting out the soft shells.

He had noticed a foxhole from afar—between the sunflowers and the plantings. The infantry was crawling in the dry grass in front of it. What were they crawling around for? The battle had moved toward the village by now, but they were still crawling around here. The foxhole looked good, it had a view of the whole field. Tretyakov waved to his men:

"One at a time, follow me!" And he ran, ducking his head into his neck.

Several bullets whizzed over his head. He jumped into the hole. And then, a round from a machine gun went over the top. He peeked out. Kytin was crawling in a serpentine motion in the grass. The butt of his semiautomatic rifle was protecting his head; the spool was on his back like a tank turret.

They piled into the foxhole and began plugging in immediately.

It was only now that Tretyakov realized why the infantry was crawling in the grass: A machine gun had them covered on the field and was keeping them there. A head would go up, the machine gun would fire from the plantings, and the movement would cease.

"Bravo, Bravo, Bravo!" Suyarov called into the phone in a frightened voice, and the echo he heard said, "Oh . . . oh . . . oh . . ." They shouldn't have stuck their noses in this foxhole. They could see the field, but so what? They couldn't destroy the machine gun. The heavy guns placed two kilometers from here would hit their own troops if they tried to get the machine gun.

"Bravo? You hear me? It's Acacia, Comrade Lieutenant!" Suyarov handed him the receiver, blinking away the sweat.

Povysenko's hoarse voice was on the line. Then the commander of the division took the phone away from him. Tretyakov could hear him ask Povysenko: "Who do you have there? The new fellow? What's his name?"

He had never seen the division commander, he knew him only by his voice.

"Tretyakov! Where are you? Report on the situation! And don't lie to me, understand? Don't lie!"

"I'm here in the field. To the left of the planting. The infantry is trapped here."

The howl of a mortar shell. They all hunched down. Several exploded above them. When Tretyakov crouched, he kept hold of the phone.

"What's going on there?" the division commander shouted. He could hear what was going on. "Where are you?"

"In the field, I told you."

"What field? What field?"

"There's a machine gun holding us. . . ."

"Are you planning to fight? What the hell do you need with the machine gun?"

"It's keeping the infantry. . ."

"I asked you a question. Are you planning to fight?"

There was a quick screech. They were shooting from nearby: *Screech—boom! Screech—boom!* He peeked out and barely had time to sit back down. It came so close he thought it would knock his head off. He peeked out. Judging by the sound, it was coming from the village.

In the field soldiers were crawling away from a fresh shell hole. One remained facedown, motionless. If that German battery were not destroyed right now, it would kill the entire infantry unit. If he could only get on the roof of the cow shed . . .

For a second he stopped breathing: It seemed that this mortar shell was coming straight at him, meant for him. It exploded so loudly that the foxhole shook.

"Do you see the roofs of the sheds?" Tretyakov shouted, deafened. He tried his arms and legs, shook off the dirt. "That's where I'll be located."

He could barely hear the question.

"Are our troops there? Germans? Who's there?"

Who the hell knows who's there? he thought. Our infantry is visible. If he could get up on the roof, he'd see everything.

"I'll be there, I'll report!"

"Watch out for—"

He couldn't make out what to watch out for; his ears were ringing. He shook his head, but that made the ringing even louder. He shouted to Suyarov to disconnect them. There was no point in sitting here. Why had he come here and dragged the others with him? They sat while the infantry lay under fire on the field. If they sat long enough, they'd get killed, too. But suddenly, now that it was time to leave it, the foxhole seemed so safe.

"Kytin! Go first."

Going first was no pleasure. But the machine gunner isn't expecting the first man; he gets ready after that and waits for the others.

"Take the spool, the phone, and make a beeline for the sunflowers!'

Kytin wiped the sunflower seed shells from his lips, wiped his hands on his knees, and grew serious. He flung his rifle over his shoulder and squinted at the distance he had to cover.

"I'm off."

He leaned his stomach over the breastwork, then flung his legs over, jumped up and ran, the skirts of his greatcoat sweeping the grass. They watched. Before he reached the sunflowers, he threw the heavy spool ahead and then followed it with a great leap into the flowers. By the time the machine gun fired, sunflower heads swaying, indicating his trail, there was no sign of him.

"Suyarov! Your turn!"

Suyarov was working hard, striking a flint against a stone. He lit up, took several drags, the cigarette shaking in his fingers. He kept sucking on it.

"Am I supposed to wait until you've had enough?"

"Coming, Comrade Lieutenant, coming. . . ."

His hands fluttered near his mouth, the stump of his ring finger jerking.

46

"Are you going to be long?"

"Coming, Comrade Lieutenant, coming. . . ."

His face was sunken and wet with sweat. He began backing away, still sitting, and protecting himself with his elbow.

Wee-oooo! came the whine from the field. *Bang, bang, bang!*

"Are you going? Are you?" Tretyakov kicked at the man, to get him up, but he rolled onto his back. "Are you? Are you!?"

Suyarov gasped in astonishment. Something exploded overhead again.

No longer in control of himself, Tretyakov grabbed him by the lapels of his coat, lifted him from the ground, and pulled him close.

"Do you want to live?" He shook him. "You want to live more than everyone else?" He felt a desire to beat him. Instead he kicked him away.

Suyarov struck his back against the foxhole wall, and blood gushed from his nose, bright red, like the juice of an underripe cherry. He stared up from the ground and lay down on his back again, his hands clawing his face.

"Live, you bastard!"

Tretyakov grabbed his gun, grabbed a large eighty-meter German spool of red telephone wire, and tossed them up onto the ground.

Someone fell into the foxhole with a groan. A green cap. Frightened, fading eyes. With dirt- and blood-covered hands pressing his belly from the side. Tretyakov saw that just as he started to run, and for a second he thought: Stay, bandage him. But he was running, the spool in his hand, the wire unrolling. The whine of a mortar shell came from the field. No shot, no jolt, just that separate, most audible whine. Bending lower as the whine grew louder, Tretyakov ran, the wire unreeling, ran faster, faster. And faster and faster, inexorably, the shell flew above him. The metal whine, aimed straight at him, came lower. Tretyakov fell to the ground. With his whole body, flattened against the earth, with his back, between the shoulder blades, he waited. And when it became unbearable, when he couldn't breathe anymore, the whine stopped. A deathly silence hung over him. He narrowed his eyes. The explosion came behind him. He jumped up, livelier than before. As he ran, he looked back. The smoke of the explosion hung over the foxhole. He reached the sunflowers and fell down. He looked again. The smoke was coming right out of the fox-hole. That was where Suyarov and the platoon commander with the green cap had been.

7

Pressing himself against the log wall of the cow shed, Tretyakov felt his way to the corner and peeked out. A bullet whizzed past his temple. He waited, collected himself. Pulling his neck into his shoulders, he ran across the empty space. Fell. The dried dirt was rich with manure, mixed in by hooves. He jumped up, knocking off the plank holding the gate, and saw Kytin crawling under the fence, covered with straw and manure. He pulled at the gate. Sheep made a rush for it.

Kytin ran in waving the wire in front of him.

"Plug in, hurry up!" He crawled up. His greatcoat was in the way. Hurrying, tearing off hooks, he tossed it down to the ground.

There was an explosion outside. A ray of sun pushed into the hay through the hole in the roof. Tretyakov climbed up on the wall again, hopped up, grabbed a beam, pulled himself up, and sat astride it. The beam was covered with a layer of bird droppings and velvety dust. Standing up on the beam, he poked a hole in the roof with his gun barrel and got out. He ran along the tiled roof in his rubber-soled shoes, holding on with one hand, and lay down on the hot tiles. A real view!

Below he saw the battle in the village. Infantrymen huddled in garden plots behind houses and then ran across the street, one by one. The dusty street was like a fatal line;

machine guns blasted it steadily, and already several men lay facedown in the dust. Nevertheless one man after another would tear himself away from a building and run headlong to fall on the other side.

Beyond the village, beyond the gardens, so close that he could make out faces in his binoculars, Tretyakov saw the mortar battery in a ravine. A big German wearing a helmet stood between two mortars and placed a shell in each one. There were two shots. A radio man got up out of the grass. Standing on his knees, he waited with his receiver. He shouted and waved his arm; a German observer, lying somewhere with a pair of binoculars, had passed an order to him.

Tretyakov banged his gun on the roof, making a hole next to him.

"Kytin! Do we have a line, Kytin?"

"Yessir!"

Kytin was fumbling in the hay, doing something with the phone. Lambs huddled in the corner of the shed.

"Call the battery!"

The division commander bothered him with questions, wanting to know where he was. He demanded that Tretyakov reveal his location with a flare, but Tretyakov had neither flare nor flare gun.

In the meantime the German in the helmet at the mortar battery was putting more shells into the barrels. He was handed them from below, and he lowered them in—left-right, left-right—tail down and then quickly covered his ears. The barrels would blast, and while the shells flew in the air, he had time to toss in the next ones, shouting something merrily and then plugging his ears. Beyond the bushes and invisible from here, other mortars fired from the ravine. The tops of the bushes shuddered, puffs of smoke flew up in the wind, and helmets appeared here and there only to vanish. The mortar battery was carrying on destructive fire, shells exploding right in the field between the planting and the sunflowers, where the Russian infantry was trapped and flattened.

Tretyakov passed along the command to open fire. There was an explosion behind him, as if it were something heavy striking the ground instead of a weapon going off. He waited for his shot with bated breath. In the entire battle, the entire war, there was only one spot in the world, and that was where his shell was to strike. Suddenly the German mortar men fell to the ground, then started to get up. But Tretyakov didn't see the explosion.

He recalculated his aim, more to the left. While he waited for Kytin's "Fire!" he saw a soldier start running across the street, his feet moving fast. A stream of bullets cut along his feet, drawing a line in the dust. The soldier fell.

"Fire!" came from below.

Listening to the flight of the shell, he tried to direct it mentally, kneeling on the roof without realizing it.

This time the Germans fell to the ground even faster, but again there was no hit. He glanced over to where the soldier had fallen. Empty. No one. But it didn't register in his mind; he saw it and forgot it.

For the third time he passed along the command, and once again it was all repeated. He had sent out three shells and not only had missed, he couldn't even find his explosions. He cut back his aim sharply. While he waited, he saw a German's head, and then his shoulders, come out from behind the shed and the wagon by the shed wall. He disappeared and then peeked out again. Tretyakov lay down on the roof and reached for his gun.

The German was out, making his way to his men. Bent over and limping hard on his left leg, he ran. Afraid to miss, Tretyakov followed with his rifle barrel. As he was pulling the trigger, the German, as if sensing something, turned around. Anxiety and fearful joy were on his face: I'm safe, I'm alive! And then his face shuddered. The German began straightening, straightening, his back straightened painfully where the round had hit, arching; his raised and contorted arms went behind him. And he collapsed, dropping his automatic rifle.

At that moment Tretyakov saw his explosion. Among the other explosions in the field, behind the battery, smoke rose from the bushes. That was a ravine—that's why he hadn't seen his hits: They'd exploded in the ravine. He changed his scope.

"Fire!" Kytin shouted below.

Tretyakov waited with the binoculars at his eyes.

The Germans in the ravine scattered, running away from their mortars. They fell as they ran, flattening out. The long, endless moment of anticipation continued. Tretyakov could make out quite clearly the abandoned firing position: cases of shells, the mortar guns upturned, the sun shining on the dusty barrels. Time had stopped. One soldier couldn't stand it and jumped up from the ground. . . . And then the explosion came from the ravine.

"Three shots at the battery—nonstop fire!" Tretyakov shouted. And while the blasts were going off and things were flying up, the roof he was on trembled beneath him.

And when the dirt tossed up by the explosions settled, when the smoke was cleared by the wind, there was nothing at all at the enemy firing position. Only plowed-up soil and craters.

He noticed something living moving on the other side of the ravine. He looked. Making it over the crest, the mortar man crawled out of the ravine, dragging himself along as if he had been run over.

8

In smoke and dust that blocked the sun, the battle raged on.

The tanks, stopped earlier by the antitank ravine, had made it across and were burning in the middle of the field. Soldiers lay across the field. In their faded shirts, they blended into the reddish field. And no one's voice—not the sergeant's, not the commander's if he were to show up here—could make them get up. Subordinate to no one now, they lay in the grass in front of the antitank ravine, as if they were still crawling. And below, brought down from the roof by an explosion, Tretyakov almost stepped on a man covered with clay. A green phone wire lay across him.

When he got out of the ravine and began running, unreeling the cables with Kytin, Tretyakov kept shaking his head, as if to get rid of the bullets that were whizzing around him. The unexpected shower of bullets made both of them hit the dirt. During one second, when he pulled his face away from the ground, he saw a charcoal-gray cloud in the sky. It stood like a roiling wall, and high in the sky doves fluttered, blindingly white. He saw one cut down by a bullet. The dove was lifted above the rest of the flock, circled, and plummeted, leaving behind feathers from its torn wing. And then, like ice in his heart, he thought, I'll be killed today! The next moment he had jumped up and was running along the field with his submachine gun in his lowered hand. The bent-over running soldiers ahead of him looked white against the black wall of the storm cloud, like a film negative.

They jumped into a trench while a cloud of dust and smoke still hung over it. Kytin plugged in the field phone. Tretyakov rested his elbows on the breastwork and looked over the field with his binoculars. The lenses steamed up, sweat stung his cracked lips and poured down his chest.

The infantry was hurriedly digging in. Among the men flat on the ground, crawling back and forth, columns of explosions shot up into the air. Rounds of machine-gun fire sounded overhead, and beyond that the roar of engines as an aerial battle moved past them. People kept running along the trench.

"Comrade Lieutenant, the Germans have tunnels underground! About ten meters deep." Kytin was chewing something. "Want some bread? They left everything behind. Go see for yourself. There's ten meters of clay overhead, no shell will ever get you."

But beyond the turn in the trench, dead Germans were piled up on top of one another. The top man lay spread-eagled, there were holes in his socks, his uniform was torn at the throat, and instead of a face there was a caked crust of earth and blood, above which fine blond hair was ruffled by the wind. Tretyakov had to step over dead Germans several times on his way down the tunnel, clutching the walls to feel his way.

Sounds were muffled down there, but the explosions made the candlelight flicker and dirt crumble from the clay roof. In the dim yellow light the bandages on the Russian wounded looked white. He saw the platoon commander. Stripped to the waist, he sat on the ground, while a medical orderly kneeled to bandage his chest. Recognizing Tretyakov, the commander lifted his balding head, which was lolling weakly, and said, "There . . . they got me again. . . . I didn't last a whole battle."

The tunnel filled with dust. The explosions were constant.

Tretyakov asked, "Sergeant, you said you had that staff commander near Kharkov. Is he here? Have you seen him, huh? I'd like to learn about my uncle." His eyes urged him to hurry, tried to help him remember.

But the platoon commander stared at the ceiling. Clay fell down onto his face. The wounded grew anxious. They felt around for their guns. Some crawled off somewhere.

Above, everything was in turmoil. As Tretyakov made his way up, he had to push through crowds at every passage. In the trench there was shoving, shouting, frightened faces.

Tretyakov peeked out: tanks. Low and with long barrels. They appeared from behind the hill with the windmill. Two tanks . . . and behind them—one, two, three more. . . . Fire blazed from the first tank's gun. The shot was so powerful that it blocked his ears up.

"Kytin!"

The telephone lay covered with dirt. The spool of cable was not there. Neither was Kytin. Tretyakov picked up the receiver. No connection.

Soldiers who had not dug in lay in the field. The tanks advanced. In front of them people flew up as if on gusts of wind. They jumped up one at a time and, crouching, ran as hard as they could. Some were gunned down.

"I'll teach you to run!" the battalion commander shouted into the phone, while an artillery lieutenant kept looking helplessly at his map. He was as white as a sheet, explaining something on his phone, not opening fire.

"What guns do you have?" Tretyakov shouted.

"Howitzers . . . one-twenty-twos . . ."

"Where's the battery?"

"There. And there." The lieutenant pointed them out on the map and looked at Tretyakov hopefully.

Tretyakov calculated the distance and relayed the order. "Open fire!"

A young guy in sergeant's stripes was hanging around for no apparent reason and regarded Tretyakov with awe.

55

"Attaboy, Lieutenant!"

And suddenly Tretyakov heard Kytin's gasping voice on the receiver, "Acacia! Acacia!"

"Kytin?"

"It's me! There's a splice here on the field. . . ."

Then the division commander's voice came on: "What's going on with you? Tretyakov! What's going on there?"

"The Germans are counterattacking with tanks! We need cover fire. . . ."

"Tanks . . . How many tanks do you see? How many do you see yourself?"

"I saw five. . . . Just a minute . . ."

Tretyakov was going to say, "I'll count," when the trench was hit and he was knocked off his feet. Clumps of dirt fell on him, hitting his back, his head, while he kneeled and tried not to vomit. Sticky saliva dripped from his mouth, and he wiped it away with his sleeve. He thought: This is it. . . . And he was amazed—he wasn't afraid.

The young sergeant lay in the bottom of the trench, his arm outflung, fingers moving. And where the battalion commander had just been shouting and shaking his cap there was nothing but a smoking crater.

Getting up on shaky legs, unable to tell whether he was wounded or not—there was no blood—Tretyakov looked at the field, the explosions, the running and falling men. Slowly, as if his own head were spinning, the arms of the windmill on the hill revolved, the bottoms covering and then revealing the advancing tanks. Sensing the inexorability of time moving, then stopping, through the noise and the roar in his ears, hearing his voice as if it were a stranger's, Tretyakov relayed commands on the phone to the division. He used his binoculars. Everything grew closer and harsher. Its caterpillar treads shining, the front tank advanced, and the windmill's arm with slats missing came down, separating it from the rest of the pack.

Another explosion. Something jerked the telephone and

pulled it over the breastwork. Grabbing it and holding it with his knee against the wall, Treytakov shouted a new command. There was a harder jerk on the phone. He turned around. A black, white-toothed face smiled at him over the breastwork.

"Nasrullaev!"

The face smiled even more, showing about a hundred teeth, all strong and white. Nasrullaev, his signalman, crawled over with two spools of telephone cable on his back. He was holding the wire he had jerked.

"Get down here! Fast!"

Nasrullaev kept smiling as if he didn't understand Russian.

"Get down, I'm talking to you! Where's Kytin?"

He reached out for Nasrullaev, but suddenly he was hit near the elbow, and his arm burned with pain. He grabbed his left arm with his right hand, not understanding who had hit him, only feeling that he couldn't get his breath. And before he saw his own blood, he saw the fear and pain on Nasrullaev's face. Then blood came out of his sleeve. Feeling weak, feeling his face and lips go numb, Tretyakov sat down on the bottom of the trench, for some reason feeling around for the submachine gun next to him.

9

The village and Yaitseva station were burning. Everything was escaping from the flames, like sparks from a campfire. Traces of bullets flew into the sky. The vehicle crawled along the field in the dark, in the twilight reflections of the flames, sinking into craters. The wounded rolled onto one another, groaning, shifting in the bed of the truck, while the engine whined as it tried to pull the truck up onto flat ground. They circled the field some more, moving away and then moving closer to the battle. Once, like a vision, they saw the windmill, burning, falling apart before their eyes, fiery pieces falling; the mill glowed like a heated wire carcass.

The jolts made blood flow from Tretyakov's throat, and he wiped his mouth with his sleeve. He would wipe and then look at the dark stain on the fabric. Of all his wounds, he felt only one at first, when he was hit near the elbow— right on the funny bone—knocking the phone from his hand. The orderly counted four other holes in him. Shrapnel between his ribs interfered with his breathing. That was what made the blood gush out his mouth. Contorted, in expectation of pain, he prepared for the next jolt, when the truck would fall into another pothole and every wound would ache.

"Oh, ow!" a junior lieutenant next him cried out. "Oh, my God, how can this be? Oh, God, let it be over soon. . . ."

They kept circling the field. There was no end to the circling. The engine whined with the strain or grew quiet. The light of the flares shone into the truck, then darkness would fall again. Time was measured in jolts and pain.

They stopped. Voices in the dark. Footsteps. Iron creaking. The back was opened. They took the wounded down one by one. When the junior lieutenant was removed, he did not groan. The voices hushed. He was taken aside and laid down on the dark ground.

A strange sergeant helped Tretyakov get down, bustling around him, offering him support.

"Lean on me, lean harder. Harder, it's okay."

Tretyakov's trouser leg, stuck to a wound, pulled away and he felt heat pouring down his leg. That meant another hole. He hadn't felt it until now. Someone small, determined, with straps on his chest came over. Tretyakov was brought to him.

"So that's what you're like, Lieutenant. We'll send you out, the docs will fix you up, you'll be back in the regiment. We'll wait for you."

Tretyakov saw the captain's insignia on his shoulder and realized that he was the division commander. He hadn't pictured him as being so short just from the voice.

"I yelled at you today." The captain frowned. "We're all nervous in battle. Don't take offense, you shouldn't."

"I didn't."

Things were swimming before his eyes. It was hard to breathe.

"You mustn't take offense, you know."

The sergeant led him forward. Barely hearing his own voice Tretyakov said, "Take me . . . over there . . ."

The shrapnel between his ribs wouldn't let him take a breath.

"Over there . . . sergeant." He pointed at the bushes.

The sergeant was trying so hard. He didn't understand

what Tretyakov wanted. He just supported him more with his shoulder.

"We're almost there, it's not far, come on. . . ."

"Sergeant . . ."

"Don't worry!"

He finally understood, hurried him over, started to unbuckle his belt for him.

"Go away," Tretyakov said.

"It's all right!"

"Go . . . please." He couldn't breathe deeply, and his voice was pathetic as a result. "Go away."

Holding on to a small tree, he swayed with it, as weak as a puppy. But he was willing to put up with that, so long as he did not have to feel shame. But the sergeant, breathing tobacco and vodka, kept saying, "It's all right!" And he took care of things naturally and without a fuss.

"What if it happened to me?" he said. "Wouldn't you help me? We have to help each other here."

And he didn't move away, he supported him the whole time. Then he buttoned his fly for him—Tretyakov didn't have the strength to resist—straightened his shirt, and then took a look at Tretyakov's commander's belt in his hands, with the star buckle.

"That's a fine belt you have there," he said shyly. "Do you know what it's like in the hospital? What comes in on you goes out on them. I've been in—I know." Tretyakov sighed; he really didn't want to part with the belt. "And if you're unconscious, you'll never find your stuff."

"Take it," Tretyakov said. The sergeant was happy and quickly put *his* old belt on Tretyakov.

"Mine's still good. Just rub the worn part with benzene."

They were leading Tretyakov somewhere again, transporting him, shaking him up. Then he sat on the ground. All around the trees wounded men lay, sat, and moved. There was a rumble in the air. Freshly bandaged men, their ban-

61

dages very white, were brought out of a nearby tent. And while the orderlies moved among the wounded, to pick the ones to be treated next, the wounded looked up at them and groaned more pitifully.

Tretyakov heard everything through the ringing in his ears. Sometimes the ringing would seem farther away, fading out. . . . With a shudder, he jolted awake. His heart pounded. He knew he must not sleep. It was like being out in the cold: If you fall asleep, you won't wake up. He struggled to stay awake. But everything in him was getting weaker. His heart was no longer beating; it was trembling. He felt life seeping away. Once he heard voices above him:

"Don't sleep, Lieutenant!"

A black shadow blocked the red sky and bent lower.

"Hey, come on. Come on, come on, get up. . . . Help me, Nikishin. There. Fine! Can you walk?"

The stiff canvas of the tent flap struck him on the face and knocked off his cap. The orderly picked it up and shoved it in the pocket of his coat. Inside, he was blinded by the light of the kerosene lamps. In the corner a man stripped to the waist held his hand up with his other hand and watched a nurse pull out a brown-stained bandage with tweezers from a black hole near his elbow.

Masked doctors were bent over the table. Below their hands was a round shaved head, and instead of a temple and cheekbone there were oily lumps of blood, an enormous wound. The doctors were digging around in it with their chrome-plated forceps, taking something out, metal jangling in the basin on the floor. The man's eyes, glistening brightly, stared ahead, separated from the pain, separated from everything. Only the foot showing from beneath the sheet trembled.

Tretyakov, stripped naked, was also trembling. The table was warm when they put him on it. The surgeon was taking a drag on a cigarette someone was holding for him. He kept his gloved hands up at shoulder level. His face was covered

up to the eyes, and when he bent down, the mask was drawn
in by his breathing, showing his mouth and nose, and then
it fell away again. They moved something dull across his
body. Metal rang in the basin. Again the seemingly dull
scalpel slid along, and his body cringed in anticipation of
pain. A few more pings in the basin. Then—the pain.

"Squeeze your legs together!" the surgeon said.

The heat went in straight to his heart and he gasped.

"Scream, let it out! Scream!"

The woman's voice faded in and out, he heard her breath-
ing next to his ear. Someone wiped his face with a wet cloth.
Once the surgeon's face was very close, and their eyes met.
He said something and Tretyakov's heart felt freer.

When they were bandaging him up, the woman offered
him a bloody piece of metal wrapped in cotton.

"Do you want to keep it as a memento?"

"What do I need it for?"

And it fell into the basin, too.

Weak and trembling, Tretyakov was taken to a ward
where he shivered half the night under his coat and under
the blanket. Every time he shut his eyes he saw soldiers
running in the dry grass, the black wall of the storm cloud
ahead of them, their shirts and the grass white. Or he would
see the foot trembling on the operating table, tense with
pain, the toes curled up tight. And several times that night
he saw Suyarov. He would squeeze his eyes tight, but still
he would see how he had beaten him, how he fell on his
back, blinking, protecting himself with his hands. That was
the last thing in Suyarov's life: being beaten. What a thing
to take on your soul! . . .

Infantry ran among soaring explosions, a cloud rose up
like a wall beyond the antitank ditch. Something moved in
it, swirling like a whirlwind. Swaying, it moved closer. And
suddenly with sweet pain in his chest, everything in Tretyakov opened to meet it.

"Mama!"

She stood on the other side of the ditch, so sorrowful. She looked at him without a word. He felt her, her breath on his cheek.

"Mama!"

Choking on love for her, glad that for the first time in his adult life he could tell her that there was nothing wrong between them, he hurried toward her. But someone was holding him by the shoulder, pulling him back. He jerked with pain and woke up. A bandaged head, like a white balloon, swayed above him in the gray dawn.

"What do you want?" Tretyakov asked, turning away; his cheeks were wet with tears.

"You were screaming. Do you need anything?"

"I don't need a thing."

He was sorry that he had been awakened. He lay there a long time. It was getting light. The ward was coming to life. The orderlies were giving out hot tea, checking bandages, changing dressings.

Outside beyond the tent flap, everything was covered with dew. The cold sun rose and stood high over the woods. The wounded men listened to the nearby battle and moved fretfully on their beds of straw covered with rain capes.

Next to Tretyakov was a commander of a battery of anti-tank guns. He had lost both arms above the elbow. Tretyakov could smell the hot metallic odor of his blood, soaking through the bandages where the stumps of his arms ended. A wounded soldier from his unit held the commander up and fed him tea from a mug while he told someone else behind him how the German tanks attacked, how it all had happened.

"The worst part is that the commander used to be a tailor before the war," the soldier said loudly, as if an armless man could not hear, either. "How will he manage without his hands? He won't be able to earn his bread without his hands."

There was something about the way the commander

looked—the white beaked nose, bulging eyes, reddish drooping mustache on the bloodless face. He reminded Tretyakov of his stepfather, even though his stepfather had not had a mustache.

The tent flap was jerked aside brusquely and several officers entered. A colonel wearing medals came first. A doctor peeked over their heads.

"Greetings, my eagles! Who was the first among you to fight your way into the German trench in the battle?" There was silence. The colonel waited. A whisper rustled over the wounded men, "The division commander!" A young and handsome soldier near the entrance of the tent sat up in the straw. Tretyakov could just see him on a poster.

"I did, Comrade Colonel!"

"Bravo! Hero!" The colonel glanced over his shoulder and his aide was already taking a silver medal for valor from the chest. It dangled from a ribbon. The colonel pinned it on the soldier. "You earned it! Wear it!"

Another man, not so good-looking, sat up. His arm, bent at the elbow, was pressed against his chest under his shirt.

"Me, too, Comrade Colonel . . ."

A medal was pinned to his chest too. No one else got up. But someone's weak voice asked from the corner, "Did we take the station, Comrade Colonel?"

"We did, my eagles, we did. Get well now. Our medicine is good. It'll return those who are capable back to the front!"

The colonel left just as swiftly as he had come, with the rest crowding out after him. The last to leave was the doctor, who looked back sternly at the wounded men.

10

The earth slipped by endlessly under the rails, the blue-gray skein of the locomotive's smoke hung on the telegraph wires, and the autumnal woods appeared and disappeared. Tretyakov fell asleep to the creak of the train, to the throb of its wheels, and when he would wake up, the wind would still be spreading the smoke on the fields, and the forest would be speeding by in the distance under the piercingly blue sky.

Snow must have fallen somewhere to the north by now; cold air came in through the door. Here, though, on land over which the war had rolled twice, once each way, the sun still warmed the soil in farewell.

When he woke up again, they were in a field. Silence. The door was rolled back and a soldier in jodhpurs sat in the opening, bare feet in the wind, the left sleeve of his shirt torn off. He had unbandaged his arm and was picking maggots out of his wound with a small stick. Another soldier stood on the ground, watching closely and winding the bandage. A third man came over, his crutches making noise in the gravel.

"Why are you taking the maggots out? They're useful, they keep the wound clean."

"Yeah . . . but do you know how they tickle under the bandage?"

The train whistle blew. The wounded men climbed back

into the car, pushing their crutches in ahead of them. Someone jumped and was pulled in. And the earth slid by again
under the rails and the smoke settled on the wires. The fields
were silent.

Tretyakov, watching from the top bunk, looked at the
beauty of autumn that he might not have ever seen again.
He hadn't lasted very long this time—just one battle, and
not even to the end of it. But he felt at peace. How many
people would be needed if the war was in its third year
already and each person spent so little time in it? Before
officer's training school he had spent some time at the front.
He had been wounded then, through his own stupidity. It
wasn't even a wound, just a bump. Of course, that had been
on the northwest front, where all the battles were of only
local significance. It couldn't be compared with this one. But
people got killed there, too, and many were left behind in
the damp, swampy woods.

The train was going uphill. A trembling black shadow of
smoke blocked the sun in the car. Through the heavy puff-
ing of the locomotive came the cheery voice of someone on
a lower bunk. Sometimes it was drowned out by the clatter
of the wheels, then it would break through again.

"They had taken off their flea-covered shirts . . . spread
them out on the table, and sat opposite each other, squashing their own fleas. *'Ein Russe kaput! Zwei Russen kaput!'* It was
so funny to watch . . . they were laughing themselves. . . ."

Tretyakov recognized the voice. The storyteller was the
fellow who had been digging maggots out of his wound.

The locomotive made it to the top, exhaled a long whis-
tling sigh of relief, and moved more quietly. The voice was
audible again.

"Battle? There wasn't any battle! Our troops had left the
night before after setting fire to the warehouse. The women
were there all night grabbing what they could. In the morning the Germans came. I was sitting on the porch having
milk and a pancake. I looked up—there they were, coming

68

on bicycles. It was hot, and they were riding in their underwear. In boots and with their semiautomatics around their necks. Some war!"

The voice faded in and out. Tretyakov, weak from loss of blood, plunged into sleep.

He saw himself under a bridge. He was in the grass, hiding behind a huge boulder while Germans rode over the bridge on motorcycles. He heard the engines roar, he saw the planks of the bridge move above him.

It grew quiet. . . . He peeked out. In front of him lay the dried riverbed, bushes. Suddenly he felt it—he didn't see it—felt eyes on him, with his shoulder blades he felt it. He turned. It was a German, standing on top, looking at him. The German was taking his rifle from his neck, his white eyelashes blinking. Feeling his legs giving out under him, Tretyakov screamed and woke up.

He lay, blood pounding in his ears, still not believing that he was alive. Why was he always so scared in his dreams? He had never been as scared in battle as he was afterward in his dreams. In his dreams he was always so helpless.

11

Early winter had already come to the Urals. The light, reflected from the snow, was white on the hospital ceiling. The patients had broken open the sealed window. They clapped their hands, shouted down, and banged their crutches on the metal windowsill.

Below in the courtyard, near the sun-warmed brick wall of the former school that was now a hospital, the school band was performing for those who were heading back to the front.

"Play one for the road!" the soldiers shouted from the window.

Tretyakov wasn't walking yet, but he could hear the sounds of mandolins and balalaikas playing a tune and a young voice rising in song in the cold frosty air.

Blind Captain Roizman headed for the window's light, clutching the headboards of beds, knocking over stools as he walked.

The band played the same song three times. The wounded men did not want to hear any other; they liked this one and they kept requesting it. The band struck up the tune again, and happy in their youth and strength, their girlish voices ringing out, the children sang it again.

Nurses ran into the room, shut the window, and pushed the men back into their beds.

"Are you crazy?! It's freezing outside. Do you want to get pneumonia?"

Later that day the one-legged orderly stumped in on his wooden leg. He had lain in these beds, gotten better, and then had nowhere to go. His house and his town were in German hands; he stayed on at the hospital. He nailed the window shut so that it would stay shut until spring; they conserved heat here. But the tune whirled in the ward till evening; the men hummed it to themselves and smiled.

In the corner, legs tucked up tailor fashion, Gosha, a junior lieutenant, sat on his bed, shuffling a deck of cards and asking for a game. Almost the same age as the schoolchildren in the band, all Gosha had managed to do in his life was to reach the front. The first time he got a concussion and was brought to the hospital. When he was better, he ran off to the front again. This time he was hit by artillery. The doctors said that maybe he had gotten another concussion. Gosha never could tell the story; he would get excited, stutter, and shake as if he were sobbing.

Every morning he would sit in the middle of his bed with a deck of cards, waiting for someone to play with him. His future was clear. Tretyakov had seen guys like him at the market near the beer halls when he had a pass from the school. Legless, they sat on the ground playing craps, swapping things they kept under their jackets, living one day at a time. Or, clutching an open pack of cigarettes in their blue fists, they stood on crutches in the cold selling one cigarette at a time. Perhaps that's why the doctors were in no hurry to release Gosha.

It was obvious that he was a heroic lad who dreamed of getting to the front and performing a heroic exploit. But his fate was neither to perform an exploit nor to die an honorable death.

On Fridays the students at the infantry school marched past the hospital to go to the steambaths. They came back singing a song. *Crunch-crunch*, went their boots on the snow. The lead singer was in the middle of the group. What if he ran out of breath and lost the tune? But he held it and his voice soared. The rest joined in for the chorus, and the boots crunched on.

The snowy street was empty, nor were there many to watch them from a window as they marched and sang. It was wartime, and whoever wasn't at the front was working for the front twelve hours a day. Once in a while an old woman's face in a scarf would appear at a window and her faded eyes would follow them down the street.

It was cold and the students walked fast. It wasn't their coats that kept them warm, it was the song and the pace: *crunch-crunch, crunch-crunch.* Sometimes kids ran out behind the column; they wanted to march, too, left right, left right! And the wounded men in the hospital would smile, as if seeing themselves in the past.

Two weeks later, when Tretyakov had gotten a little stronger, they performed another operation on him. They removed small fragments from his arm, sewed up the nerve, and wrapped his arm in cellophane. "Wrapped it like a candy for you," the surgeon said.

The operation was done under local anesthetic, and they left an ampule of morphine with the nurse for the night, when the pain would be at its worst. He walked up and down the corridor until dawn, but he refused the shot. There was a senior lieutenant in their officers' ward, also an artillery man, whose hands had been shattered by exploding bullets. While they transported him in the truck, and then the train, they kept giving him morphine so that he would sleep and let others sleep. Now he begged for morphine from the nurses, traded for it, lied, whined shamelessly. Tretyakov decided it was better to bear the pain rather than turn into an addict, even though the nurses laughed at him and said that you don't turn into an addict from one shot.

73

Toward morning the nurse took pity on him and gave him half a glass of vodka. He drank it, lay down, put a pillow over his head, and slept soundly.

When the white light of the snow was in the room, white branches swayed outside. Two cots away a young girl in a white coat was sitting next to the bed of a Captain Atrakovsky, who had an Order of the Red Banner. He was the only one not to keep his medal under the pillow; instead he wore it on his shirt under his robe. He was gravely wounded; a piece of a mine was lodged in his brain. The doctors said that he could live his whole life with that fragment or he could die unexpectedly at any moment.

Dominoes clicked on the lunch table. Blind Captain Roizman's slippers scuffed across the room as he bumped into the beds. The girl spoke quietly; Tretyakov couldn't make out all her words.

"I can't forgive myself. . . . I didn't understand. . . . He was so nervous. 'Have you forgotten?' I only realized then that he only had a half hour left. . . . He smoked one cigarette after another . . . wanted to say . . . . When I got there, everybody was on the platform already. . . ."

Tretyakov had the feeling that she turned in his direction.

"He's asleep," the captain said. "He had surgery last night."

Oddly, Tretyakov felt hurt that she didn't ask about him, that he was only a hindrance to her conversation.

The bed was jolted; that was Roizman. More scuffling sounds as he moved away. The girl spoke more softly.

"And then, when the whistle blew, his mother began kissing him. How she kissed him! On the neck, the back of his head, his forehead. . . . It was only then that I understood what was happening. I was glad that he had come by and that he had seen me with my hair down. But he was going off to die."

Tretyakov wanted to see her face, but all he saw was her braids and her large gray soldier's boots under the stool.

Suddenly he remembered where he had seen those boots before. When he was being led down the steps of the hospital train, two people crawled out from under the train: a girl all wrapped in a shawl—it was very cold—and a young boy in a black leather hat. Happy and flushed with success, they looked around to see if anyone had noticed them. They had a full bucket of glowing, still usable coal that they had picked up on the tracks. He noticed the girl's soldiers' boots, just like these, enormous. Maybe it was the same girl?

"Fellows," Roizman called. His arm was raised and the gray flannel sleeve had fallen down. He was feeling the edge of the window. "This is the window, right?"

The dominoes stopped clicking. Silhouetted against the light, Roizman touched the window, touched the frame. His eyes, uninjured, clear and unseeing, looked around the room in bewilderment.

"I can see the light. There . . . there it is. . . ." With trembling hands he caught the light in the window.

12

From the corridor near the rebandaging room Tretyakov could see the railroad tracks and the station, its huge windows white with frost. Once in his childish simplicity he had thought those windows were the way the little engine that went for a ride on its own had gotten out.

He was four then, and his father was still with them. His father had told him not to fall asleep but to watch their things while he and his mother went off somewhere. Tretyakov sat on the suitcase and imagined that the station manager had fallen asleep in the corner by the stove and that the engine pushed through the windows with its steel chest. When his father returned, he got the baggage, took Tretyakov by the hand, and they went into a large room bright with electric lights. People were chatting happily, cigarette smoke rose to the ceiling, and amid all that noise and festivity sat his mother, alone at a table covered with a white cloth, waiting for them. Everything was exciting, different from home. It was the first time he had ever eaten in the middle of the night. And the meal wasn't served by his mother, but by a man with a white cloth over his arm. He was amazed at how quickly they cooked there. Mama often spent half the day at their primus stove, while the man with the white cloth just went away, cooked, and came back with everything almost immediately.

Whenever there was a blizzard, he thought about his father. His mother sent the last food parcel to his father just before the war, and his father's last letter, from *there,* the camps, had come even earlier.

He could not forgive his mother for having another husband when his father was still alive, *there,* or that anyone at all could be her new husband. He couldn't stand watching her take care of him, or the way she looked at him sometimes. Unconsciously Tretyakov looked for the most unpleasant things about his stepfather, and he never did call him by any name. *"You're* wanted on the telephone." "There's a letter for *you."* But most often he used Lyalya to communicate to his stepfather: "Tell *him* somebody's asking for him."

Lyalya, the little fool, grew attached to Bezaits. She didn't remember their father. Once he saw her feeding cookie crumbs to a photograph of their father. She was sitting on the floor by the bed, whispering something and putting the crumbs near the lips on the picture.

He was the only one to keep his father's name, Tretyakov. And he stole all the pictures of his father, even the ones where his mother was in the pictures too. Now they, along with Lyalya's letters to him at school and his mother's letters, were all in his field bag, left at the front in the sergeant's van. Even as he was leaving the front he thought, "But I'll return to the regiment." As if one could predict anything in the war.

The one-legged orderly moved from window to window down the corridor. He would stand, take a look, remove a nail from his mouth, and hammer it below the windowsill. Next he'd take another look, stand a bit, and hang a bottle from the nail. Then, flexing his stiff fingers, he would lay a wick made of washed bandages along the sill so that whatever water melted from the windows would not drip on the floor but go down the wick to the bottle.

His mother used to hang bottles at windowsills too. In the mornings the glass would be frozen up high and sometimes

Tretyakov would warm a coin in his hands and press it against the ice. Then he'd warm it again and do the other side. Heads, tails, heads, tails. A lost world. Everything before the war seemed like a lost world now.

The station doors opened and people piled onto the platform, all bundled up to the eyes. Covered with steam, the train pulled into the station. Ice rimmed the roofs of the cars; icicles dripped down the white, translucent windows. And as if the train had brought the wind with it, the snow blew from the station roof and swirled across the platform. In the snowy whirlwind and the steam, people rushed from door to door along the length of the train. They always ran along with their bags and small children, but all the doors were closed. There was no room for anyone.

The orderly was also looking out the window. He carefully spat the nails into the palm of his hand.

"They should get that Hitler here! He's sitting where it's warm and cozy. And our people have to suffer like this. . . . And with children, too." He shivered as if he had felt the cold.

Tretyakov thought his conversation stupid. Taking out his anger on the orderly because he too felt sorry for the women who were being chased away from the train, he said, "Well, what do you think, that if some Hitler wants a war, it starts? And if he wants, it ends?"

His own officerlike tones made him straighten up in his robe.

The orderly looked sadder and grimmer.

"Well, I didn't want the war," he muttered to himself as he went to the next window. "Or did you think I found two legs excessive?"

Tretyakov watched him go, with his one shoe and his peg leg. You can't sew his leg back on and you can't explain things. He couldn't explain it all to himself, either. At school, from a teacher, he learned how wars started and he got good grades—the inevitability of war under certain circumstances was understandable and simple. But there were no easy explanations for what he had seen in these years. It had happened so many times before—wars would end and the same people who had been annihilating each other lived together peacefully and exhibited no hatred toward each other. Was there no other way to achieve that peace than killing millions of people? Did peace first need people to be forced into echelons by battalions, regiments, platoons? To hurry, to rush, to suffer hunger and other deprivations on the road? To march fast, just to arrive at a battlefield and be scattered, cut down by machine guns, smashed by explosions, and left there because it was impossible to take them away and bury them?

We are fending off an invasion, he thought. We aren't the ones who started the war. The Germans came to our country—to kill us and destroy us. But why did they come? They lived quietly, then suddenly no life was tolerable to them except destroying us? And if they are doing it only under orders, that is one thing. But they fight determinedly. Have the fascists convinced them? What kind of conviction is it? In what?

Grass is born and inevitably dies, and grass grows thicker on fertilized soil. But surely man does not live just in order to fertilize the earth; why does life need so many mutilated men to be suffering in hospitals?

No one person changes history by his will. It's just that it's easier for people to comprehend the incomprehensible that way: Either it occurs independently of them, or some individual makes it happen, someone who knows what ordinary mortals do not. But that's really not it at all, and sometimes all the joint efforts of humanity are not enough to change the course of history.

Before the war he had read something that astonished him. The invasion of Genghis Khan had been preceded by years of especially good fortune. The rains had fallen on time, the grass grew incredibly tall, the horses bred bountifully—and all that good fortune gave impetus to the invasion. Perhaps if there had been several years of drought and things had gone badly, there would not have been all that horror and the history of many nations might have been quite different. But perhaps it doesn't take so much to knock the wheel of history out of its rut. Maybe it's enough to put a small stone in the path?

But once the wheel has rolled free, crushing people, crunching bones, then there is no choice. There is only one thing to do: to stop it, to keep it from rolling over more lives. But could it be avoided?

It was pointless now, however. It wasn't the time for it. The war was on, the war against the fascists, and he had to fight. That was the only thing you could not pass on to anyone else. But you couldn't keep yourself from thinking, even though it was pointless.

Tretyakov and the orderly watched, each from his own window, as the train rolled off, leaving people at the edge of the platform. The last car swayed from side to side, the whirlwind of snow covered its tracks.

As usual, after dinner, they went to the ward to kill time. Platoon Commander Starykh and blind Captain Roizman were playing chess. It was over their hundredth match, but Starykh never lost hope that he would win. They sat at the table opposite each other and the ambulatory patients stood around them. Atrakovsky stood too, holding his robe with his left hand. He had walked carefully across the room, afraid to set off the pain, and stopped, watching with everyone else but somehow apart from the rest. Tretyakov had heard that in 1941 Atrakovsky had been taken prisoner and had escaped. In 1942 he was surrounded by Germans and got out. And if, after that, he received the Order of the Red Banner, the man must have done something fantastic, for people did not get that decoration easily. Now life barely held on in him; it could break off at any moment.

When everyone was in bed, they talked about their wounds—who was wounded where and how, and Tretyakov suddenly remembered.

"I knew I was going to be hit that day."

He had thought that he would be wounded or killed when he saw the dove struck in midflight. It had been an omen. But he had forgotten about it during combat and remembered it only now.

"How did you know ahead of time?" Starykh asked suspiciously.

"I just knew."

But he did not tell them about the dove—he was afraid they'd laugh at him.

A few days later, in the evening, Tretyakov saw Atrakovsky by the window in the corridor and walked over to him. He wanted to ask him about that girl: Who was she? Would she come again? Instead, he said, "Look at the snowstorm!"

Nothing could be seen outside except the snow right next to the window flying upward. Cold came from the window.

"A blizzard," Atrakovsky said.

There was surgery going on in the operating room next to them. The light was bright, and silhouettes showed through the frosted window.

"The infantry is in foxholes right now. . . . There's nothing worse than fighting in the winter. And in the spring." Tretyakov laughed. "We're lucky."

A shadow appeared, vague in the blizzard. Both of them, in their hospital robes, were reflected in the window.

"You don't know how lucky you are," Atrakovsky said. "The limits of luck. That's a defense mechanism of the young: not to understand everything. Just one word would have been enough. . . . Not even spoken, to agree silently, and your whole life . . ." He spoke without changing expression. It would have been impossible to tell that he was not talking from a distance. "Death in combat would seem marvelous compared to dishonor."

Tretyakov's heart contracted. He *would* ask him about his father! Atrakovsky might know things the others didn't. But he didn't ask; he just grew pale. His father wasn't guilty of anything, he knew that. Nevertheless, when it came to his father he felt a shameful mark upon himself and an emptiness arose around him.

A nurse in a white gauze cap rushed out of the operating room and—*tap, tap, tap*—ran down the corridor. The blizzard howled outside.

13

The evening that Tretyakov and Atrakovsky stood by the window in the corridor, and the snow swirled outside, and the yellow electric light in the frosted windows of the operating room seemed warm, and the nurse in a white coat ran out and down the hallway—that evening they amputated the leg of an actor from the local theater. They were still standing there when they brought him out. The surgeon walked by, controlled but agitated, and gave them a professional look. Then they brought out the amputated leg. It was bent at the knee and missing the foot.

The actor had been entertaining the troops and had been wounded by a bomb. None of the officers in Tretyakov's ward had ever seen any actors at the front. They toured, but they were always somewhere else, at the airports, in the rear. The actors always said that they had been at the front, and they believed it themselves. When they got home, wearing their gifts of white sheepskin jackets, they boasted to their friends, but it made real front-line soldiers laugh. And that must have been why the story of the actor losing his leg was told humorously, as if there really were something funny about a man losing his leg.

About three weeks later, just before New Year's, the local troupe came to the hospital to perform, and their comrade who had lost a leg lay on a stretcher in front of the stage.

The concert had begun when the school kids, who were

also going to perform, burst into the corridor. Tretyakov, who was sitting by the door, heard them, waited for the act to end, and went out into the hallway. The children crowded around in white coats, all talking at once.

"But dogs don't bite in the winter!"

"It wasn't even barking, that's the curious part."

"And why Sasha?"

"Really, why her?"

"Listen, what if it's rabid?"

"Sasha, don't bite us!"

"Sure, you laugh, but I don't think it's funny. Look at my stocking, at the big hole. And it really hurts terribly." The girl they called Sasha was laughing, too, to keep from crying. She stood on one foot, the nurse was looking at her other leg, and everyone was crowded around them.

Sasha. . . . Her cheeks were glowing from the cold. In the fresh snowy air they had brought with them, Tretyakov was very aware of the smell of the medicine, the hospital food, the poorly ventilated air breathed by so many sick people. He could feel that smell coming from himself, from his flannel robe, washed so many times.

Feeling someone else looking at her, the girl raised her fluffy eyelashes, so thick that they made her gray eyes look black, and looked up with all the animation that was in her. Then a shadow seemed to cross her face. Something closed inside her, not letting a stranger into her life. Then she looked up again with interest, but Tretyakov didn't see it. He was already on his way back to the ward.

Only a few men who couldn't get up were there. At the table Captain Roizman was shaving by feel under the light. "Is that you, Tretyakov?" he asked, recognizing his step. "Will you fix my temples?"

"Let me try."

Roizman felt around on the table until he found the shaving brush and lathered up his cheek. Tretyakov dunked the razor in the glass of warm, soapy water and wanted to bend

86

over, but the wound in his side wouldn't let him. He tried crouching, but the wound in his leg interfered. Roizman waited, cheek turned up.

"I can't get down to you. Stand up."

"Just a minute."

Between them they had three healthy arms and two seeing eyes. Roizman stretched the skin near his temple, and Tretyakov with the dangerous straight razor in his hand breathed near his bony face.

"Hold it. . . . Hold it. . . . Here it comes." He stepped back and took a look. "Just a little over here."

Then he did the left temple. Roizman stretched the skin with his other hand, over his head. His eyes were right in front of Tretyakov's. They followed him; they seemed to see. But they didn't meet at the nose when Tretyakov moved close.

"Do you recognize me, Comrade Captain?" he asked, wiping the razor on his knee.

"I thought there was something about the voice," Roizman said hesitantly. And faced him.

"Remember, at school you came into class, the student on duty gave the command, and when you heard his roosterlike 'Tenshun!' you called the platoon commander over and said, 'Comrade Lieutenant, I never want to hear that student giving commands again.' "

"Yes, yes, yes," Roizman remembered joyously. "Was that student you?"

"Yes."

"Wait, that was in . . ."

"I can tell you exactly. The attack at Stalingrad began on November nineteenth. The fronts were joined on the twenty-third. We were at the train station in Moscow and heard the report. We were going from the front to the school and heard it. Then we were drinking in Kuibyshev for three days. Our sergeant was from Kuibyshev. We spent three days at his house, drinking beer by the bucket. We would have partied some more but we ran out of food. So that was the end of November. And in December, in the very first days, I gave that command before you. You taught us artillery."

'Yes, yes, yes . . ."

"And in late January or February you left us."

"February third."

"I remember. You went to the front. But your leg didn't bend at the knee from an earlier wound, as I remember. The right one? You had a cane."

"Yes, yes, yes," Roizman said, smiling and nodding. Then he asked, "You must have been hurt when I said that?"

"Then I was," Tretyakov answered honestly. "But now it makes me happy to recall it."

"Well, did you learn how to give commands?"

"They made us spend hours on the field in pairs. Walking toward each other: 'Attention! Right! Left! About face!' I'll have that for life."

"There was something about your voice from the beginning. . . ." And Roizman nodded, smiling, thinking his own thoughts.

Tretyakov thought his. There's something repulsive about me, he thought, and pictured that girl looking at him and frowning. Something about me turns people off, I know it.

After a smoke in the corridor, he went back to the auditorium. All the seats were taken. He stood in the doorway and watched an actor portray Hitler. With a pasted-on mustache and bangs combed down onto his forehead, he screamed and gibbered like a monkey. The audience laughed, banged their crutches on the floor, shouting, "More!" They wouldn't let the actor off the stage, as if the real Hitler were giving them this pleasure. For some reason that made Tretyakov ashamed of them and himself. He didn't know why he was ashamed, but there was something in that simple mockery that diminished Tretyakov in his own eyes. Maybe it was just his mood.

The girl in the felt boots and white coat came out onstage, and two boys with mandolin and balalaika came out after her like an honor guard. They sat down on the edges of their stools, she nodded and the boys nodded in return and struck the strings, and she began to sing. Tretyakov lowered his eyes quickly, as if afraid. He stood that way, eyes downcast cheeks tingling, getting more upset. The song was about something he had seen more than once.

"You're waiting for a word from your love, you don't sleep, missing me, We'll win the war, and I'll come galloping to you. . . ."

It didn't matter that he hadn't seen it just like that or that it was a different war, fought not on fiery warhorses but more simply and more horribly; it didn't matter because the song excited him and made him sad. Besides his mother and sister there was no one waiting for him or missing him; a girl like the one in the song would ask if he had been brave in battle. Standing in the doorway, looking down at the floor, he listened to the end of the song.

Then he went back to his bed and thought. He twisted and turned and couldn't get comfortable; he couldn't even tell if it was his soul or his wounds that bothered him. And he recalled Lieutenant Afanasyev, in the regiment on the northwest front, who had killed himself disgracefully over love. No one had seen or heard from him for two days, and a rumor had started that he had gone over to the Germans. Then they found him in his long underwear and shirt, a kilometer from the firing line. He lay in the melting snow in the forest. His right hand, which held the pistol, was all scratched, and his temple had powder burns. They pitied him and condemned him. To shoot yourself at the front, where so many were killed every day. . . . If you don't want to live, they muttered, there are the Germans—go kill them. And the woman over whom he had shot himself lived with the division commander; he had his own dugout. She wore padded trousers and men's boots and her voice was hoarse

with cigarette smoke. That brave handsome lad killed himself over her. But Tretyakov thought: What if he didn't see
her the way everyone else saw her? What if he knew something completely different about her?

14

A few days later Sasha returned. Tretyakov was sitting on the windowsill in the corridor and Sasha was telling him about the young man whose name had also been Volodya and and who had died two months ago. "His friend wrote to me. He had seen Volodya's tank go up in flames. Everyone had gotten out of the tank, Volodya, too, when the tank started burning. But he lay down and fired at the Germans so that the others could get away. Maybe if he had run right away, too. . . . But he was commander of the tank."

"You can never predict that," Tretyakov said, for her sake. And he thought, She's lucky if it really happened that way. He could have burned inside the tank.

"You can never predict," he continued. "I had a soldier who refused to get out of the foxhole. Something happened to him. He was afraid; he couldn't get out. The ones who did get out are alive, and he died. A direct hit on the foxhole. That's rare, actually, a direct hit. But that was his fate."

"Volodya had just turned nineteen." She looked at Tretyakov, comparing them. "Are you twenty yet?"

He nodded. He was still nineteen, but he wanted to seem older in her eyes.

"He had just turned nineteen. When he got word that his father was killed, he kept it from his mother. He only told Zhenka, his kid brother. They both loved their mother very much. She is a large, beautiful woman. Such a Russian face, with a touch of Gypsy in it. The sons look like her. Both have hazel eyes and thick, curly hair."

She looked at his hair; he was standing in front of her and she had to look up. His hair wasn't black; he didn't even know what it looked like now that it was growing back in. Lyalya, the silly girl, his loyal sister, who considered everything about him to be perfect, would put the end of her braid up to his hair and say, "Mom, why isn't my hair like Volodya's? Why is he handsome, and I'm not pretty?"

Sasha's eyes were glistening nervously, the way they had been when she was talking to Atrakovsky. "His mother had begged him, 'Please, don't go. You have the right by law not to go. You can stay, I can arrange it.' But he was as firm as steel about it. He hid the fact that he had asthma from the medical board, and forbade his mother to tell. He told her, 'If they don't take me, know that I will consider you my enemy for life.' Now she can't forgive herself."

Nurse Tamara Gorb walked by, carrying a hot autoclave wrapped in towels. She looked at the two of them. Sasha jumped down from the windowsill and stood in her felt boots until the nurse went by. She came up to Tretyakov's shoulder. Her two ash-colored braids, each as thick as an arm, hung below her waist. Short-haired Tamara had looked at the braids as she passed.

Tretyakov took a cigarette from the crumpled pack of Bokses in his pocket. He didn't want to smoke as much as he wanted to cover up the fetid hospital smell he felt coming from his robe.

"I'll go get a light," Sasha said simply.

"Someone will come by soon," he said. And a patient, bent double, appeared at the end of the corridor. Tretyakov went and got matches from him.

As he was coming back, he passed the open door of the spine-injury ward, where Tamara had gone. On the nearest bed a patient was looking at himself in a hand mirror. He was flat on his back and moved the small mirror around, pulling clumps of hair on his head, smoothing them, trying to neaten himself up. He was even younger than Gosha. A shell fragment had gotten him in the spine and he was paralyzed from the waist down.

Tretyakov finished his cigarette before he got back. Sasha helped him light another. "Volodya Khudyakov smoked like this, too, one after another, at the train station," she said. "He'd drop one and light another, over and over. His mother can't forgive me for letting him go off so sad. He was standing in the doorway when the train started, and at that moment I got so scared for him. I felt that something was going to happen to him; I could see it in his face."

"You think so now," Tretyakov said. "Nobody can ever know ahead of time."

"No, you can have forebodings."

"You can, but only one in a thousand comes true. And it's for the better that people don't know what will happen to them. If they knew, they wouldn't be able to fight. This way, everyone has hope." He saw that she wanted to believe it, but that she would still blame herself. The living always feel guilty about the dead.

Tretyakov stood by the window and watched the school children meet under the streetlamp in the courtyard of their former school, watched them walk across the courtyard in a group. Sasha was wearing a fur coat that was too tight; she had outgrown it. Tretyakov waited for her to turn around, to look up at the windows, but somebody late was trying to catch up with them, and they all ran faster. Then they stopped to let a train go by. Sasha did not turn around. He stood and watched as they crossed the illuminated tracks, jumping across the rails.

"Volodya!" Tamara Gorb called him.

Tamara was in her thirties and she had this crazy crush on

Kitenev, and now she would unburden herself again. He came over, carefully stretched out his wounded leg, and sat at her desk.

"Yes?"

Tamara looked at him as her small, round, black eyes filled with tears. The tears spilled from both eyes, just brimming over. "Why is he so mean?" Tamara said, wiping the tears that fell on the desk with a piece of gauze. "Why does he treat a living person that way? I'm not asking for anything. I came to give him his medicine, and instead of him, his coat is under the blanket. . . . Well? I was the one who got him that coat in the first place; is that what I got it for? It's twenty-four below. What did he go outside in?"

Tamara was hopelessly plain. But when she cried, her tear-filled eyes were incredibly beautiful. The next day she would see Kitenev and he would flash a smile at her, and Tamara would forgive and forget.

That seemed to be his role here: People unburdened themselves to him, he listened. They talked to him as if he had already lived a long, long life, or he was a stranger on a train to whom you could tell anything because he'd get off at the next stop and you'd never see him again.

He went back to the room. As usual, there was a chess game on. Captain Atrakovsky was walking from corner to corner, carefully coughing into his hand.

The light in the room was low, making it almost impossible to read in the evenings, even though he didn't feel like reading much in the hospital. Nothing in books seemed real. But Atrakovsky read. He read everything: newspapers, books. The last time he noticed Atrakovsky was reading Shakespeare's *King Lear*. Tretyakov's hands shook when he picked it up; it reminded him of home. His father had Schiller and Shakespeare next to each other in the glass bookshelves. Heavy dark-green volumes, leather bound, the illustrations covered with tissue paper. He had read them when he was still in school and had looked at the pictures before he could read. He started reading *King Lear* again but didn't understand it. He understood the words, all right, but he couldn't see what the tragedy was. Had he grown so dumb during the war? Or had he not understood something more important before? Yet for so many centuries people have been feeling sorry for the king as he raves mad on the plains. As a kid, Tretyakov had suffered along too.

He read the stage directions: *Offstage, the sounds of battle. Lear, Cordelia, and their troops pass with drums.* That was where he stopped. The sounds of battle. There were dead men lying in the field there, backstage of history. And they killed each other for no good reason. The king did not divide up his estate properly among his daughters, and men died. But people didn't feel sorry for them, as they weren't human. But for the king . . .

Gosha and Starykh sat apart from the rest in the corner of the room. Gosha, as usual, sat cross-legged in the middle of his bed. Starykh was leaning toward him from his bed, scratching his tanned bald head and speaking softly. Gosha was the old-timer in the ward, and his bed by the window was considered the best. He kept moving toward it a long time ago until it was free. Now he had no place farther to go. No one was waiting for him. He was an orphan. He didn't even remember his parents. He was happy to go to war and had run off from the hospital after his first concussion. But he was afraid to go back to the rear, back to the real world. The most important part of his life was running off to fight at the front.

Tretyakov lay down on top of his blanket, settling all his parts comfortably: his wounded arm, wounded leg, wounded side. Atrakovsky's shadow moved along the wall. Why was he sorry for everyone today? He pitied Gosha, he pitied Tamara, and he felt such pity for that girl with the braids.

15

The days were getting noticeably longer, and on one sunny late January day they saw Gosha off. He had breakfast with everyone in the room. Then he left and came back in his uniform. They were in their robes and hospital slippers, and he was in boots and overcoat, holding his hat in his hand, glowing.

Gosha looked at his empty bed from the doorway. The bed had been stripped; the pillowcase was taken off.

Kitenev rustled a newspaper and then stuck a package wrapped in it inside Gosha's coat. "For a certain civilian!" Gosha started stuttering and wanted to pull it out of his coat, but Kitenev held his wrist.

"Take it, take it, you're going out into the world. Come on, it's nothing!" It was money they had collected, money Gosha had lost playing cards in the last few days. He had no luck at cards; maybe he'd be lucky in love.

Through the melted spot in the window Tretyakov could see the snow falling in the windless air. Each snowflake settled slowly. Gosha went out to the gate, his rubber soles leaving a neat track. At the gate three roads lay before him: straight, left, right. He just stood there, unable to make a decision.

The ward grew cheerless without Gosha. Everyone plunged into his own thoughts. In the middle of the day Starykh managed to get drunk somewhere, and he shouted that they were all fakes and he was the only real wounded man there. He waved his crutch about and his eyes were crazed. They forced him to bed.

Closer toward evening the door to the room opened and two orderlies carried in a stretcher and put a new patient on Gosha's bed. The wounded man lay quietly, wearily opening and closing his black eyes. A bullet had gone through his brain, in above one ear, out above the other. He was alive, but very, very quiet, very docile.

In the corridor, Tamara was bringing out a part of the patient's skull on a piece of cotton from the operating room. It looked like a walnut shell.

Tretyakov awoke in the middle of the night. It was dark. The new moon's greenish light came in through the icy windowpane. Everything was as usual, but he felt more and more anxious. Then he understood; the patient in Gosha's bed had died.

Tretyakov got up and went over to him in his underwear. The pointy nose stuck out from under the bandages. A dead man's face, yellow-green in the moonlight. Eyes shut forever in the black hollows. Tretyakov bent over him and stood, looking. The eyelids fluttered. His eyes opened, alive, damp with sleep, and looked at Tretyakov.

"Thirsty?" Tretyakov asked; he had almost lost his voice.

He fed him carefully from the tip of the pitcher, watching the man swallow weakly. He felt grateful to the man for being alive. The man blinked twice, to say, Thanks, I've had enough.

"Get some sleep. Call me if you need anything. Don't be shy."

Tretyakov slung the robe over his shoulders and went into the corridor to have a smoke. It was cold there; the wind had shifted and was blowing from this side. A southwestern wind from the front. But it didn't carry the voices, the shots, the explosions this far. The war roared only at the movies here. Later boys ran around with stick rifles after seeing the newsreels. But wherever the front had passed, even the kids didn't play at war.

A nurse was sleeping on duty, her cheek on a stool. He went back inside the room; into the fetid warm air and lay, chilled, under his blanket.

When the schoolchildren came to the hospital the next day he saw right away that Sasha was not among them.

"They took her mother to the hospital," the fellow who played the mandolin told him. Not even knowing why, Tretyakov asked where Sasha lived, how to find the building.

After dinner he made up his mind. Without looking him in the eye, he asked Kitenev, "Captain, lend me your overcoat tonight."

"Aha!" Kitenev said merrily. "Look what a diet of oatmeal can do!"

They all helped Tretyakov get ready. Only now did he realize how helpless he was with just one good arm. He couldn't put on his shirt; he couldn't wrap his foot cloths. Starykh, with his own leg in a cast, wrapped his foot cloths. Even Atrakovsky helped; under his pillow he had a few newspapers, which he read and marked, and he selected two, after giving them a last read-through.

"Wrap his feet in these."

"Don't," said Tretyakov, embarrassed to accept such a sacrifice. "It's not that cold out."

Kitenev, like the Lord God who had created him, stood above them all, and said, "Just wait till I get released. I'll leave you everything, my overcoat, my cape, my boots."

In proper military manner one of them went out first and scouted the halls. Then Kitenev led Tretyakov out of the hospital. Beyond the gate, in the light-blue snow under the cold scattering of stars, he had his first breath of cold air since they had locked him up in the ward. The fresh cold air went deep into his lungs; it even made him cough. He walked and was happy, happy to be seeing the winter, to be walking on the snow, to be going to Sasha's.

The icy snow creaked under his heel. When he took deep breaths, his nostrils stuck together. His wounded arm was under the coat, bandaged to his chest—it was warm there— and he warmed his ears with his other hand. He wiped the tears from his cheeks; the wind was squeezing them out of his eyes, eyes grown unaccustomed to the cold.

Two men on patrol, walking together and making their rifle butts sway in rhythm, passed under the streetlamp at the train station. He waited behind a building. What if they asked him who he was and where he was going and why? He looked like a runaway. A military coat without insignias, an empty sleeve held by a belt—where could he have come from? Rather than risk explaining, he waited around the corner.

The patrol walked past slowly, the most important people on the square. They were headed for the station, to warm up. While he was waiting for them to pass, a white cloud rolled in from a locomotive, surrounding him in damp warmth and coal smoke. The station door slammed. The patrol was inside. Tretyakov came out and, keeping to the shadows, crossed the tracks. There they were, two four-story houses, just as he had been told.

At the porch he suddenly grew wary. He had been hurrying, joyful; now all his determination evaporated. Above the kitchen curtains he could see the ceiling, stained by soot from the kerosene stove. The door was unlocked. The entry was full of stamped snow and just as cold as the street. Two apartment doors. A stone staircase led upstairs. Which one?

One door was covered with sacking for insulation, the other with old black Leatherette. He straightened his coat under the belt, adjusted his hat, and knocked on the Leatherette. The cotton batting under it muffled the sound. He waited, then knocked again. Steps. A woman's voice on the other side of the door.

"Who is it?"

Tretyakov coughed into his hand and said, "Tell me, please, does Sasha live here?"

Silence. "Which Sasha?"

He suddenly realized that he didn't even know her last name. He wanted to say, "the one with the beautiful braids." Instead, he said, "Her mother was taken to the hospital. . . ."

"So what?"

Why didn't she open the door? "Please call Sasha. I'm here from the hospital to talk to her on business."

Another long silence. The chain rattled and the door was opened a crack. A plump, bare arm under a warm shawl, a puffy face. From behind her came the smell of kerosene.

"We were told that Sasha's mother was taken to the hospital," Tretyakov said, as if he were speaking for the entire Red Army. He tried to placate the woman with a smile, standing so that the dim light would show him from head to foot, that there was nothing to be afraid of. The woman peered at him warily and did not take the chain off the door.

"Who are you to her?"

"That need not concern you. Does Sasha live here?"

"Yes."

"Please call her."

"She's not here. She went to the hospital."

He hadn't expected that she might not be home.

The woman suddenly took the door off the chain. "Come in, why let all the cold air into the house?" He came in. The hazel eyes in her bloated face looked at him with curiosity.

"Did Sasha go there a long time ago?"

"Not so long ago, but quite a while."

And she kept looking at him, with more and more pity.

"Is it far from here to that hospital?"

"It's not really a hospital. The hospital is in town. This is just a barracks, for contagious people. When Sasha came home from school, they had taken her mother away. Oh, she was really bad, she was. I told her, 'Sasha, wait, my Vasilii will come home from work, we'll ask Ivan Danilych.'"

"Who's Ivan Danilych?"

"Ivan Danilych?" She was astonished that anyone might not know. "He's the military commander, my husband's older brother, that's who. 'Sasha, wait until then and we'll ask. . . .' She didn't say anything and wouldn't eat a thing. She paced the house like a mouse. It was dark, but I heard her go out. She couldn't wait."

"How do I find these barracks?"

"Go the easy way. Along Myagotin and then turn right on Gogol. And then straight. And then right on either Pushkin or Lermontov. And then go along the woods. . . ."

"And that's where the barracks are?"

"Not right away. First you come to the cemetery. Tobol's off to one side."

The cemetery was a good landmark. Everyone could tell him how to get there.

"They're right after the cemetery. There's nothing after that, just a cliff."

"Thanks," Tretyakov said. He had at least a vague idea of where to go. When he was at the door, he turned and said, "If Sasha gets back before I find her, don't tell her I was here. It'll just worry her. . . ."

But he could tell from the look on her face that she would tell Sasha before the girl was through the door.

16

They didn't even wake him for breakfast. Half asleep, Tretyakov heard voices, and Kitenev saying, "He's been having trouble sleeping. Up half the night . . ."

He woke again from the bustle. In the middle of the room by the table several people were crowded together. He heard glass clinking on glass, the sound of pouring liquid. They were pouring something.

"So . . . who's next?" Kitenev asked quickly. "Atrakovsky can't. Roizman!" He took Roizman by the sleeve, placed a glass in his hand that looked murky in the light. "Come on!"

Seeing the glass, Tretyakov recognized the smell and sat up in his bed.

"Why are you drinking so early in the morning?"

Kitenev looked at him. "You should get some more sleep. Our troops are approaching Berlin, and you're just getting up."

"No, really, what's up?"

They poured him a glass. "Drink! Questions later." But they told him right then and there. "Avetisyan just had a daughter."

They informed him that last night Avetisyan had begun talking. He'd waited for it to be quiet and then spoken up. Practically his very first words were "I just had a little girl." And the enormous eyes in the thin face asked, Will my daughter have a father? The consensus seemed to be that he would live. And they decided to celebrate those two events.

In his sleepy state he didn't realize right away that Aveti-syan was the senior lieutenant who had been shot through the head, who had scared him one night. He raised the glass to show that he was drinking for him and drank, trying not to grimace, not to lose his standing with the grown men. Starykh watched the bottom of the glass go up, and even swallowed, helping him along. Then Starykh was given a glass filled to the rim. And even though they were all in a hurry and kept looking over at the door, he did it sternly; it was a sacred moment. He looked them over with clear eyes and concentrated.

"Well!" He nodded to himself, exhaled, and drank, his eyes narrowing with pleasure. Then he turned blue, coughed, and his eyes rolled up. "Bastards! Who put water in there?"

A roar of laughter. Kitenev wiped the tears from his eyes.

"Don't be so greedy. When I pour for someone else, you're drinking it up with your eyes. You really shouldn't have any at all. In our unit we had a strict rule: four glasses, three with alcohol, one with water. Only the man who poured knew who got what. We'd drink. And you could never tell from the faces who had which drink. But this one, he coughs from water." He poured equal amounts for him-self and Starykh from what was left in the decanter. Just two glasses. "Here, don't cough!"

Then they quickly washed the decanter and filled it with tap water. Kitenev wiped the outside dry with a towel and put it back in the middle of the table, and then he spread out the chessboard. People playing chess, a useful mental occu-pation. They turned on the radio loud.

Because Tretyakov had been up half the night, the alcohol made everything more vivid, as if he had developed new vision. The winter light seemed special, and the white sky outside, and the snow that drifted against the window.

Every tree branch was twice as thick because of the snow— it swayed on itself.

He looked at everyone and at the same time saw himself and Sasha walking along the road last night with the moon shining on them. Maybe it hadn't happened.

He really had had no hopes of finding the barracks. Why was he going? Who was expecting him? He turned back several times, then went on again. He pictured Sasha seeing him and being overjoyed. But Sasha did not recognize him. She was standing alone in front of the barracks, the snow was blowing down from the roof, and the porch light seemed to be glowing in smoke.

"Sasha!"

She turned, shuddered, and backed away.

"Sasha," he said, and walked toward her. Then he realized he should stop. "Sasha, it's me, it's me. Your neighbor told me your mother is sick."

Then she understood, recognized him. She started to cry, wiping the tears with her mittens.

"I'm afraid to leave. She's so thin, so thin, just skin and bones. She doesn't have the strength to fight."

He protected her from the wind with his back and got so cold that his lips couldn't form words anymore. As they were walking home through town, Sasha asked, "Do you have anything under your coat?"

"Yes."

"What?"

"My soul."

"You're not wearing anything else?" Sasha was horrified. "Let's go faster."

He could have been walking on wooden legs. He could no longer feel his toes. There was something swollen and numb in his boots. Sasha's felt boots trod softly next to him, and the moon was shining, and the snow glistened. It *had* all happened. . . .

Starykh came over and sat on his bed.

"You didn't get frostbite on your feet?"

"No, just cold."

"Thank him for that." Starykh pointed to Atrakovsky, who was reading his papers. "You can go out in the coldest weather even without felt boots." He wiped the sweat brought on by the moonshine from his brow. "You young people need teaching. . . . Remember while I'm still alive!"

A little while later, by the window in the corner, Starykh sat on Avetisyan's bed as he had on Gosha's, talking to him loudly, as if he were deaf.

"Daughter—how do you say that in your language?"

Avetisyan responded softly.

Starykh moved his lips in wonder, trying to pronounce a new word.

"Well, that's all right. You can say it that way, too."

Tretyakov's heart was so full with the memory of last night that he felt richer than any of them.

17

Now Faya, the neighbor, opened the door for Tretyakov as if he were family, and if Sasha wasn't home she invited him in to wait. Her room was always hot and white with antimacassars, tablecloths, and coverlets that hung and lay everywhere. By the wall stood the bed with a luxuriant pile of pillows.

Never taking her feet out of soft boots cut in the back to fit her calves—not the rock-hard factory-made felt boots, but soft ones sent from her home village—Faya sat amid scraps of fabric sewing something small or crocheting a tiny bootie. Faya's soothing voice and the metallic flicker of her hook made Tretyakov drowsy, and the heat made his ears tingle.

"There's so many evacuees here, it's terrible!" Faya sighed. "They have lots of money, and all the prices have gone up."

Her flannel robe could no longer cover her belly, and her thin hair, shining under the lamp, was combed back, the bun held in place with a semicircular comb. It was so quiet in the room that it was impossible to believe that somewhere the war was on.

"Whatever is brought to the market, the evacuees buy it up. They grab it right out of your hands. Money's gotten cheaper, and people are getting rid of it."

Faya talked, and Tretyakov thought his own thoughts.

"Evacuees"—that word didn't even exist before. They used to say refugees in the last war. Once he was walking down Plekhanovskaya and suddenly there was herring for sale. It was the very beginning of the war; they were just bringing in ration cards. This was without cards, the way it was before the war.

They had rolled barrels down the street to the sidewalk, set up scales; and the saleswoman in a wet apron was selling herring by weight. She pulled them out of the barrel by their heads and slapped them down on the scale. A line sprang up immediately, and more and more people came running, pleased with their luck.

It was hard to remember that now, to look back. The Germans were in Minsk then, and so many had died and were dying, dying every hour, yet people were happy to get herring! And he was happy too, imagining how he would bring it home, herring bought without a ration card!

He listened to the conversations in the line: "Will there be enough for everyone? Should I get in line? Or not?" And others held conversations about an enormous tank battle somewhere in the south, over a thousand German tanks destroyed. Someone who knew firsthand added authoritatively, Now the Germans will go back. . . .

Then a horrible wind blew on the people in line, like ashes from a raging fire. Horse-drawn carts and pedestrians moved down the street along the trolley tracks. The newcomers were not locals. They were dressed every which way, some in silk dresses, some in fur coats in the middle of summer, sooty children peeking out of the carts. They were refugees, the first refugees they had seen there. The war had chased them ahead of it. The line moved aside to let them get at the herring first, but all they wanted was something to drink.

Someone's felt boots crunched in the snow outside the window. He and Faya listened: Faya's husband? Sasha? Each was waiting. The front door slammed. Sasha. Rosy cheeked, her shawl icy around her face, she saw him and looked happy. "I saw Mother. They don't let you inside, but I looked in from outside and saw that her throat was bandaged; she looked so miserable in the window. She can't talk; she nods to me from the window."

The hoarfrost melted on the shawl and in her hair and glistened in the warmth. He hadn't ever seen her look so beautiful.

She untied the shawl, took off her coat, and ran off to the kitchen to wash up. He hung up Sasha's coat, still warm from her body, next to his greatcoat, and looked at them together. Standing in the middle of the room, he waited. Sasha came back, wiping her face, the towel muffling her voice.

"Mother and I slept together and I didn't catch it, but now whenever I come back from there, I scrub and scrub and I still have the feeling all those germs are on me."

She took a pot wrapped in a jacket out from under a pillow, where it was kept warm.

"Let's go light the stove." She picked up some wood that was drying by the oven and took it out to the corridor where the stove was. "I heat the place at night now, with mother gone." She was crouching as she tore the bark from the logs to use for kindling. "I'm not home all day anyway, but at least this way I go out into the cold from a warm room."

"What do you eat, Sasha?"

"Don't worry. We have potatoes."

They started the fire together. The smell of birch smoke and light from the stove filled the corridor.

"Don't smoke yet," Sasha said, peeling him a cooled potato.

"I don't want one," he said. "I've had dinner."

"How could anyone not want a potato? I think the smell alone is . . . It's our own potatoes, not store bought."

A large peeled potato sparkled sugary in the firelight.

"Here."

He held it in his hand until Sasha had peeled one for herself.

"Do you like them baked? I adore them. And if there's also milk . . ." She took a bite. "Eat. I embroidered a dress for a milkmaid around here; it took a whole month. I'd get up on the bed with my feet, one eye on my textbooks, the other on the embroidery. Cornflowers on gray linen, on the sleeves, the front, and the hem." She outlined it in the air, and he pictured her in that dress, cornflowers and her gray eyes. "She brought us a whole quart of milk. . . . I forgot the salt!"

"It's good without the salt."

"I think so too. It's a marvelous variety. We planted just the eyes—can you imagine—and got huge plants. One bush yields half a bucket."

She ran to the room and put the saucer of salt on the metal plate in front of the stove. The red flame danced on their faces on the light metal plate. They were sitting on a low bench, dunking the potatoes in the salt, pink in the reflected light.

"You were completely different when I first met you," Sasha said. "And your face was different."

"How?"

She laughed. "I can't remember anymore. Just the face of a stranger. No, at one time it wasn't a stranger's face. You know when? They were bandaging my leg, and you walked down the corridor. You walked past and I watched you. You pretended to be just passing by. I felt sorry for you. But that still wasn't you. I might not even recognize you. Remember how we sat on the windowsill?"

"You looked through me."

Sasha said nothing. The reflections played on her features.

"You know the first time that you were the way you are now?" She looked at him.

"When?"

"The night you came to find me. I didn't see it then. I remembered the next day and thought that you got chilled and were probably sick. You were so cold in your coat and you protected me from the wind."

They talked and looked into the fire, and what they saw there belonged to the two of them.

"Remember, I asked if you had anything on underneath? And you laughed: 'My soul.' Your lips could barely move. I worried the whole day that you had gotten sick."

"You were frightened of me that night."

"I got scared when you came out from behind the barracks. You didn't see yourself; you don't know how scary you looked. You were covered with snow, like a wolf. I even imagined your eyes were shining. I was terribly scared."

The front door slammed. Vasilii Danilych Pyastolov, Faya's husband, came down the corridor. The metal buttons on his railroad uniform were white with hoarfrost; it was cold today. Vasilii went by without a nod; he was very dignified when in uniform. He came out of his room a different man, in a vest, worn boots, an old hat, and carrying an axe. He was headed for the woodshed.

Seeing her peeling another potato, Tretyakov lit a cigarette from the stove.

"Wait," Sasha said again.

"Enough. I'm full. When I light up, I can't eat anymore."

"You can't?"

"I can't."

"You lie so honestly. And you have the eyes of a saint."

"I'm not lying."

"You're not? When you're done smoking, you'll eat this one."

She cleaned one for herself.

"When we dug up the potatoes in the fall, I thought we would never eat enough of them."

The still-damp birch branches hissed in the fire, yellow

sap boiling on the ends. Fending off the heat with one hand, Sasha moved the branches, her fingers glowing, backlit by the fire.

"Mother wasn't like this at all before the war. But now the least thing makes her defenseless." She looked into his eyes. "My mother . . . Mother is . . . German. . . . Do you realize what that is? A German when we're at war with Germany. But she was born that way; it's not her fault. And she isn't really German. Her grandmother was Russian. It was her grandfather who took all the children secretly to Finland to baptize them as Lutherans, before the revolution. He would put them in a basket and take them so that their grandmother didn't know. If not for that, Mother would be listed as a Russian in her passport. But with her passport where can she go? We wouldn't have left Moscow for anything. But Father was very worried about her. He wrote to his sister, Aunt Nusya, from the front, telling her that we should be together, we should go into evacuation together. And after he died, Mother kept saying, 'If anything happens to me, at least you'll be with Aunt Nusya. Otherwise, you're completely alone.' She has this fear all the time; she's going to feel guilty for everything the Germans have done. It's like a mark on her. You can't understand that if you haven't been through it yourself."

But he did understand. They didn't have Germans in their family—his mother and father were Russian—but his father had been arrested. Four years before the war, "German" didn't mean what it meant now, but he had the mark on him then, and he felt it. Sasha was even closer to him now.

"I have this guilt about my mother," she said. "Our first spring here was so horrible, I don't know how we survived it. Father died, and we sold everything we had brought with us. I'd drink a glass of warm water in the morning and go take my exams. And one time . . . I'm so ashamed! When Mother was so sick, I just couldn't stop thinking about this. . . . See, I got two days' worth of bread on our ration cards. For mother and for me. I came out of the store and I couldn't control myself. It smelled so good! I went back in and asked the saleswoman to cut off a piece. She lopped off a huge piece with her big knife, and I ate it. I couldn't help it. Mother knew, of course." Tears rose in Sasha's eyes. "Mother had a dependent's card. I was working evenings after school, and she was my dependent, and I took bread away from her, and she's the kind of person who would give away the last thing she had. We hadn't sold all our things then, and it was terribly cold. People would come begging, evacuees, with children. . . . She would give them something secretly and then act guilty. 'Daughter, you and I live in warmth. . . .' "

Sasha got up and went into her room. When she came back, her face was angry, her eyes dry, her cheeks burning.

"It's still cold in there," she said. "Let's have tea here."

She brought cups and took the sooty teakettle from the stove. It stopped blocking the light and made the corridor brighter. They sat facing the stove, and their enormous shadows flickered behind them on the wall, fading into the shadows near the ceiling.

"And do you know how she got sick?" Sasha said. "Aunt Nusya's boy, Lenya, got diphtheria. Mother convinced Aunt Nusya not to send him to the hospital, because he would die there. She managed to get serum somewhere and took care of him herself. She was afraid I would get infected, so she kept washing me with bleach. And then she got it herself."

Tretyakov walked under the shaggy winter sky that evening, under the wires thick with frost. Walked and thought. He thought about Sasha, the war, the blood that had been shed at the front for three years now.

Sasha's great-grandfather took children to be baptized, carrying them like kittens in a basket. What was the connection? There was one, an invisible one; everything is connected to everyone. If Tretyakov had agreed to stay on with the staff as Lieutenant Taranov had, he would never have met Sasha. One sees the connections only later.

A light illuminated the snow, casting his shadow far ahead. Tretyakov looked back. The blinding light was hurtling toward him along the track, sucking in sparkles of ice from the darkness.

He got off the track. A heavy train rushed by, pulling the icy wind behind it. Freight cars, platform cars, tanks on the platforms under canvas, guards in felt boots on the platforms turned away from the wind, platforms with cannon, cars, platforms, guards—everything flashed before him, hurtled by in the noise, in the clatter of the wheels. In that swirling snow, in the snowy blizzard the last car flashed by. It raced off to the front. And something of Tretyakov went with it, torn from his heart. The emptiness was palpable.

18

"Well, we've lived together nicely, shared the hospital gruel. It's time to have a sense of honor. Otherwise you can forget how to fight sitting around here," said Kitenev, his blanket up to his chest.

They had changed the linens in the ward the night before, sheets and shirts, and he lay high on the pillow in his clean hospital gown, arms behind his head, the white sheet turned down over the blanket. He stretched, straightening his elbows, and his yawn brought tears to his eyes. "You'll listen to the radio without me, learn what's going on in the world. When I was in the hospital in the Ukraine . . ."

"You said you were never wounded," Starykh jumped in.

"I wasn't. I was buried in a bombing. In the Ukraine they'd turn on the radio first thing in the morning. It was wonderful to hear: knocked down, shot down, destroyed, etc. . . . . We'd start counting what the Germans were losing. They never had that much in the first place!"

"You weren't wounded, but you were in the hospital."

"Yes, but I wasn't wounded."

"Isn't a concussion the same thing? There isn't anyone in the infantry who fought and was never wounded or hit."

"I didn't have a concussion either. I was buried by dirt!" Kitenev said with dignity.

The months flashed by in the hospital, but each day was long. So Kitenev tried to get Starykh's goat as early as possible in the morning. It was easy to get. And they bickered because they were bored.

"You were buried by dirt. . . . And if they hadn't dug you up?"

"They wouldn't have had to bury me another time. . . ." Kitenev turned on one side, propped up his head, and looked at Tretyakov.

He was quietly bending and unbending his wounded arm on top of his blanket. The first time it was being bandaged, the doctor said, "Do you want your arm to be crooked?"

"Of course not."

"Then keep using the joint, or it will mend that way." And even though it hurt at first, and the bandage would get soaked with blood, he did not want to be crippled for life.

"Well?" Kitenev's eyes were light, as transparent as water. Tretyakov waited.

"I don't know. Should I leave you the overcoat as an inheritance or not? Maybe you're just wasting state property. Looks like it's a waste." Laughter shone in his eyes. "How are things going?"

Tretyakov smiled and waited.

"I'm asking how your moral and political situation is."

"Cheerful."

"What a lad he used to be!" Kitenev put the pillow behind his back and sat up higher. "When they brought him here, I thought he was a girl. Pure eyes, pure thoughts, and all directed at combatting the enemy. And after this time with you guys, look what's happened to him. He picked it all up from Starykh. Don't learn from him, Tretyakov. He's bald. Incidentally, you owe your life to your bald spot, Starykh. You covered it up because you were embarrassed. If you'd had a pompadour, like some soldiers, you wouldn't have put on a helmet, would you?" Kitenev ran his fingers through his wavy pompadour, which had grown out considerably during his hospital stay. The nurse spoon-feeding Avetisyan with a gruel of buckwheat groats was listening to Kitenev with such pleasure that she missed the patient's mouth and stuck the spoon in his ear.

"Come on, squeeze my hand!" Kitenev offered Tretyakov his hand.

The boy looked at the muscles playing along his forearm. "Why?"

"You ask a senior officer why? You're told to squeeze, you squeeze! Maybe you're just pretending to be sick."

Laughing, Tretyakov squeezed as hard as he could with his weak fingers.

"That's it? Are you that weak? Try it with your right! No, you have strength! Try it with the left once more? Harder!"

"That's it."

"What's it?"

"That's as hard as I can."

Starykh hobbled over, crutch under one shoulder, and threw himself down on the bed, holding the crutch. His face showed he was dying to tell one of his stories. "They brought this guy to the medical board and his hand was like yours, it wouldn't unbend. They bring him in, see, and tell him, 'Unbend your arm.' 'I can't.' They try to force it down. They can't. They're going to send the guy home. He's done fighting. But an old surgeon knew what to do. 'Show me the way it used to be.' 'Like this!' And the guy unbent it. Watch out, Tretyakov, when they ask you, don't fall for it. Those doctors are catching on now. . . ."

The doors opened and two men in white coats came in. "Volodya!"

"Oleg!" In an open white coat and with a bandoleer across his chest stood his old classmate Oleg Selivanov, looking at him and smiling. The administrator was smiling too, regarding them both paternally. The whole ward was looking at them.

"How did you find me?"

"Completely by accident." Oleg sat on the edge of the bed, covering his plump knees in tight jodhpurs with the skirt of his coat. Military uniform, shoulderboards, bandoleer, belt. But behind the eyeglasses the same meek, homey eyes. Tretyakov remembered Oleg at the blackboard in school, sweaty with shame, covered with chalk.

"Oleg, you really look like a boss."

"I can't believe you've been here this long and I just found you last night. Came across you in the files. . . ."

"Can you imagine, Captain, we were at school together?" Tretyakov said.

"It happens," Kitenev said, and got up, putting on his robe.

"Oleg, how come you're here?"

"I am here."

"Here?"

"Here." And both felt the silence of the room.

"Let's go have a smoke," Kitenev said loudly. He and Starykh went out. The hospital administrator went out too, giving the room a final look. Atrakovsky rustled his newspaper on his bed, one arm behind his head. His bare elbow with sunken blue veins did not seem alive.

Oleg wiped his glasses with the hem of his coat and blinked. Tretyakov remembered vaguely—either his mother or Lyalya had written to him about it—Oleg had been drafted with the kids from his class, Alyosha, the Eliseyev brothers, Boris and Nikita, and sent off somewhere in uniform, but then Oleg returned. His father had intervened. He was a well-known gynecologist in their town, and had Oleg classified unfit for combat because of his vision.

"Do you know whom I met at the market here?" Oleg put on his glasses. "Sonya Baturina's mother, remember her? Sonya had bandaged your head in military training class. I think she had a crush on you. She was killed, did you know that?"

"Was she in the army?"

"She volunteered. You remember the feelings in the early days."

"But I saw her in August. Those weren't the early days!"

"Are you sure?"

He was sure. He had seen Sonya Baturina at the very end of August. Someone was selling asters. Sonya said, "Look, asters! They're so blue!" He had bought a bouquet for her. Right by the Petrovsky ramp. They stood on the bridge. Sonya leaned back against the rail, fluffed up the asters, looked at them. The swift water, murky with clay, flowed beneath them, and their two shadows on the bridge seemed to be floating toward them.

"No one's ever given me flowers before," Sonya said. "You're the first." And looked at him, holding the bouquet under her chin. He was astonished at how blue her eyes were. Yellow pollen was all over her chin and the tip of her nose. He wanted to get his handkerchief, but it was dirty. He wiped the pollen carefully with his hand, and Sonya looked at him.

"I wonder what you'll be like after the war, if we meet again." That meant she already knew she was going to the front, but didn't tell him because he, a young man, wasn't in the army yet.

"Sonya's mother came over to me at the market; otherwise I probably wouldn't have recognized her," Oleg was saying. "This whole part of her face . . . No, this one . . . Wait, I'll remember." He shifted on the bed so that his other side was to the window and thought awhile. "This side. She had come over from this way. This whole side of her face was twisted and her eye stared as if it were dead. Paralysis of the facial nerve. I visited her later and she read me Sonya's letters. Very sad. . . . Hey, do you remember how we used to play soldiers on my balcony? You had a Japanese army, and I had those Hungarian hussars. Remember how beautiful those hussars were?" Behind the glasses on his broad manly face, children's eyes in which time had stopped peered at Tretyakov. They looked at him from that long-ago life when they were still immortal. Adults died, old people died, but they had been immortal.

Later, In the corridor, shaking Oleg's enormous hand, Tretyakov said, "Come back," but he secretly hoped that Oleg would never come again.

Starykh immediately asked, "A pal?"

"We were at school together. He located me."

"A big man." Starykh looked around joyously. "The homeland needs him in the rearguard."

"What do you know? His vision . . ."

". . . is bad!"

"If you must know, at night, he can't . . ."

". . . tell the front from the rear!" Starykh's ending made everyone laugh. "Too blind! This guy's as bad as the one we transported in 1942. Just when the Jerrys were moving on Stalingrad . . . I don't remember the station. . . . The hell with the name. There was a train on the tracks, with guns. There were women, children, some were getting on, some weren't being taken. There were tears, screams, shouts. They got into our freight cars. It's not allowed, but you can't leave them behind. And then this chubby citizen, like your pal, pushes on with his suitcases. They pushed him out. 'Comrades, Comrades, what are you doing? We need me.' "

"Liar!" roared Kitenev, laughing hilariously. "You're making it up!

" 'We need me!' "

19

They saw Roizman off. Watching him feel his way with his stick, his unsure foot seeking the threshold, Tretyakov pictured him once again the way he had been: proud, on unbending legs, shaven cheeks shining, his gaze cold.

The nurse brought in a man to replace him, leading him by the arm. He was bent, sickly, jaundiced, unhappy with everything. Drafted in the fall of 1943, Captain Makarikhin still hadn't made it to the front; he was still battling the doctors in various hospitals. He settled in right away.

"I won't crowd you if I take this shelf?" he asked Avetisyan, who didn't even move his jaw. He just blinked with his enormous eyelashes. "Fine," Makarikhin agreed, in Avetisyan's stead, and took over another shelf. He sniffed the pillow all over, holding it out at arm's length, shook out his mattress, sending dust all over the room.

"All they want is to send you out in the line," Makarikhin said, punching the lumps out of the mattress. "They don't care if you're able to or not." And soon he was walking around the beds, telling everyone under which article he could get an exemption.

"You're eleven B," he said, pointing to Tretyakov. " 'Limitedly acceptable, first degree,' which in peacetime means invalid of the third group."

You're an invalid yourself, thought Tretyakov, who had never had that insulting term applied to him, and he hated

Makarikhin from that moment. Starykh looked up when Makarikhin had gone out to demand something from the nurses and said, "It's quite possible he won't get to the war in time. 'I'd give my life for the homeland, but I won't go to the front.' He's one of those!" For a long time he shook his bald head, which was on his shoulders, and not rotting in the ground, only because he put a helmet on.

At lunch Makarikhin ate, chin trembling, slurping the stew. "Thieves," he said, breathing hard. "They steal half the food from the kettle. In our reserves regiment they checked up on the cook—he had stolen so much in two weeks! And the bastard laughed, and said, 'I take this much in two weeks, but I get this much in a day.'" It was an old saw, everybody had heard it, but Makarikhin was telling it like a true story. "Think how busy the cook is here. He has to steal for the bosses. And for himself. And his family."

"Listen, Makarikhin!" Kitenev called. He looked up from his bowl, eyes glazed with eating. "It hasn't affected your legs, has it?"

"I don't understand."

"You can walk normally?"

"For short distances. In general, of course, I have flat feet, one, and two, I have varicose veins."

"Short distances."

"Short ones?" Makarikhin took hold of his knee and stamped his foot on the floor. "That's all right."

"Then go—" and Kitenev told him where to go and what to do. And added: "And don't delay."

Makarikhin looked at everyone, silently picked up his bread and bowl, and went over to his bed.

"You'll get bored here without me," Kitenev said two days later, dressed in full combat uniform, with shoulder straps and boots. He signed out of the hospital in the evening, instead of the morning, as was usual, so that he could spend the night in town. Tamara Gorb was nervous and dropped things all day. She wept and then looked up with wet, flowing eyes. Kitenev was spending the night with her.

Now there were only three of the original roommates left: Atrakovksy, Starykh, and Tretyakov. And Avetisyan had become one of the group by now, even though he still hadn't spoken since that first time. All three felt quite temporary —their time was coming too.

"Move to my bed right away; you'll be next to Atrakovsky," Kitenev said, helping Tretyakov move, and slipped the overcoat under his pillow. "Use it, it's yours now." They were sitting knee to knee. Kitenev took out a flat flask. And when they had a farewell drink, Starykh's face suddenly fell.

"Infantry, what's the matter with you?" Kitenev laughed, feeling emotional himself, slapping Starykh's back. Starykh frowned and turned away. "You used to brag that you'd get there first."

"We'll all get there."

"Ask to be sent to our front; we'll fight together. They won't give you a platoon—you have a head wound. But you'll be able to handle a division just fine." They were joking, but they knew that they would never see each other again in their whole lives, no matter how long or how short that would be.

That same evening Tretyakov wore his inherited coat and went to see Sasha. Faya showed him where the key to her room was and then bragged, "Ivan Danilych is coming to dinner tonight."

Faya was washing potatoes in the kitchen, shoving them into the pot. Her face was even more swollen and had developed brown stains—over her eyebrows, and on the upper lip, so that the blond fuzz was visible. She noticed his look and grew embarrassed. "Oh, I just don't know what will happen. I have such bad dreams. Last night," she said, waving her arm as if to chase it away, "I saw a rat. And a huge

123

one, hunchbacked, with a naked tail. Oh, how I screamed! 'What's the matter?' my husband asked. I scared him. My heart was leaping out of my throat."

"Was the rat gray?"

"I think so."

"That's it. Faya, you're going to have a son and a daughter. It's a sure omen."

Faya grew pink. "Are you teasing me?"

"No! You'll write to me when the babies come. We have a man at the hospital." He cracked up.

"And I fell for it," she said. Faya wanted to get mad, but couldn't. Tretyakov was so much fun, and at least it wasn't boring with him around.

He had come to show off to Sasha. He had both arms in his shirt today. He saw himself reflected in the window, not in a hospital robe, but belted, tucked in, and he liked the way he looked. So he came over so that Sasha could see him too. Faya's pot holder caught fire and she put it out, pressing it against the stove. She looked at the door and whispered, "Sasha's mother is German!"

"I know."

"She confessed?"

"What is there to confess? What has she done wrong?"

"But we're at war with the Germans."

"Sasha's father fought against the Germans. He died in the war."

"That's what I'm saying! Every house in the city has buried someone at war. The people are angry!" She gave him a warning look. And then she whispered, as if to tell him a deep secret. "If you didn't know, you'd never suspect. She was a good woman, hardworking. Oh, it's so terrible, what's going on in the world."

Suddenly she noticed that his arm was in his sleeve. "What's this? You're not off to war, are you?'

"Shh, Faya! The enemy will hear!" She looked around

before she got it. She shook her head happily. "Won't Sasha be pleased?"

And she went back to her room, while he stayed in the corridor. Waiting.

The front door banged, and something heavy was plumped down in the kitchen. Sasha, wrapped up in a shawl, was dragging the coal bucket. She saw him and smiled. "I just knew you would come. I was walking along and thinking, he must be waiting for me." She looked so happy.

He took the bucket from her. "How did you carry this? It's so heavy!"

"I ran! So they wouldn't take it away."

"Were you crawling under trains again?"

"That's where I got it." She sounded so much like Faya they both laughed.

Sasha saw his arm. "Are they discharging you? Are you all healed?"

"No, not yet!" He admitted it. "I just wanted to show you."

He saw her looking at him in a different way that evening. When the stove was lit and they were sitting together, Sasha asked, "Do you resemble your mother or your father?"

"Me? I looked like my father. Lyalya looks just like Mother. Too bad my photos were in my field bag, or I'd show you."

"Is Lyalya younger?"

"She's a baby. Four years younger." Sasha saw his face grow kind when he talked about his sister, saw his gentle smile. The flames danced on their faces, and birch smoke came from the stove. Voices grew louder in the neighbors' room.

"I wasn't worried about you at all," Sasha said. "It's all superstition, I know. But when you have no control over things, you begin to get superstitious. They say that if a son resembles his mother, he'll be lucky. Volodya Khudyakov looked just like his mother. Maybe that's why I wasn't worried about you, because there was so much time ahead! And now I see your arm . . ."

"Know this, Sasha," he said. "Nothing will happen to me."

"Don't say that!"

"I promise. Believe me. If I make a promise, I keep it."
Faya appeared in the corridor and called Sasha into the kitchen. He sat by the stove, watched the fire, stirred the logs, and poured some coal on them. It crackled and smelled of locomotive. Gradually blue tongues of flame came through the coals.

Sasha came back, looking happy and embarrassed. "Let's go to their room."

"What will we see there?"

"They're inviting us—we can't say no."

"So we can listen to Comrade Major make jokes? Somehow I can miss that."

"We won't stay long. Come on, they'll be hurt." He saw that she wanted to go for some reason that she wasn't telling him. He got up, adjusted his uniform. "If the major puts me in the stockade, will you bring me parcels?"

"I will!"

"Remember, you're the one who took me there."

As usual, it was very hot in Faya's room. He could smell sauerkraut—there was a bowl on the table. He hadn't had sauerkraut since before the war, at home. There was also the smell of bacon. Only the smell.

Faya began bustling, seated them at the table. "Have some tea!" The brothers sat, both red, both with greasy chins.

"Here's his hand, take a look," Faya said, and picked up Tretyakov's crooked left hand to show to Ivan Danilych. He looked with his laughing eyes.

"The left?" And Tretyakov noticed that his right hand, which lay on the table, was in a black glove and the arm looked like a stick.

126

"Together you two would have two hands," Vasilii Danilych laughed. "Your left and his right, perfect!"

"Right!"

"He's been a lefty all his life, as if he knew this would happen. Father would take away his spoon and yell, 'People eat with their right hands, their right hands!' And he'd get into trouble at school, too. But when his right arm was blown off in the Finnish war, his left one came in handy."

And the military commander said, "Right!" His round eyes laughed sleepily.

"He holds more in his left hand than most people do in two!" Vasilii Danilych praised his brother, who permitted it. "You need a hundred doctors? He'll have them the next day. How long is each trained in the institutes? About five or six years? He'll give them twenty-four hours to get ready—and they're ready. You need two hundred engineers—he'll put two hundred in front of you!"

Ivan Danilych listened, wheezing, breathing through his nose, laughing sleepily. He shook his head. "Look and see if you have something you can set up in front of us."

Vasilii Danilych looked in his buffet and pulled out a pint of vodka. "It used to cost three rubles and fifteen kopeks before the war! Six for a liter, three fifteen for a half. A pack of Kazbeks used to be three fifteen."

"Did you ever smoke Kazbeks?" his older brother asked.

"That's why I remember, because I didn't smoke them. They were too expensive. They took the fifteen kopeks as a bottle deposit. Think how much more it's become now. A hundred times more!" he said, pouring into small pony glasses, which Faya had washed and was now putting out again, shaking them dry. "More than a hundred times!"

And now, apparently, appreciating its real cost, Vasilii Danilych wiped a drop from the neck of the bottle and licked his finger.

Tretyakov felt funny about accepting the drink. Back at the hospital whatever was brought in was common property. Here he felt he was drinking someone else's. But it wouldn't have been nice to refuse.

They drank. Faya put some sauerkraut on his plate. "Have some to follow the liquor."

"Thanks." But he pushed the plate toward Sasha. She blushed. The brothers laughed.

"I love the way they do it: He drinks, she eats." Faya, pretending to be angry, tossed some more on the plate.

"I don't want any, Faya, really," Sasha said.

"Should I put it on separate plates?"

"No, we'll eat together." And they were together, even though they tried not to look at each other. Each tried to push more food toward the other. Faya, trying to seem even angrier, came over and picked up his hand with its crooked, unfeeling fingers and showed them to Ivan Danilych.

"How's he going to fight with this hand?" She moved his fingers like rags. "What can he do with it?"

He took his hand away and made a joke. "My work is mental, Faya. It's not the infantry, it's the artillery. You can do it without hands."

"What do you think?" Faya said heatedly. "It's all legal, legal you know! Ivan Danilych, if it's not legal, don't ask him!" And the younger brother confirmed this with his big brother's favorite word, "Right." Now Tretyakov understood why they had been invited, what Faya and Sasha had been whispering about in the kitchen. A silly woman, Faya. Once one got to know her, you saw that she was nice. If he could just get some firewood for Sasha. But at least now he could drink that shot of vodka with a clear conscience.

Ivan Danilych, from whom Faya and Sasha were waiting to hear the word, picked up his wooden prosthesis in the black glove with his healthy, red, beefy hand and moved it to a more comfortable spot. Maybe the reason he was still alive was that wooden arm. And it had definitely protected his kid brother from service at the front.

"Well, Vasilii, do you have any more or what? If you do,

pour it." Vasilii Danilych poured, and it was just enough for three glasses. The big brother picked up his glass with his big fingers, and said vaguely, "When a man has shed blood for the homeland, he has the right! And he will!" And he gulped down the vodka.

Out on the street, Sasha asked guiltily, "You're not mad at me, are you?"

He smiled like an older man. "You and Faya are sweet. I couldn't figure out why you insisted we go there. Conspirators . . ."

"But why is it always the best ones who die? My father, and poor Volodya. He died at nineteen. Don't be mad that I keep talking about him. I can't even see his face anymore. I remember it, but I don't see it."

They reached the hospital. The lamppost at the gate illuminated the snow around it.

"Why are we here?" Tretyakov asked.

"But they'll be looking for you."

"I'll find them myself. Sasha, they won't send me any farther than the front. Let's go somewhere else first. You're not too cold?"

Happy, amazed that they hadn't thought of it sooner, they quickly headed back, the snow crunching under his steel-tapped boots.

20

After the street and the cold air the stuffiness of the ward seemed unbearable. Tretyakov shut the door carefully behind him and tiptoed in. When his eyes had adjusted and he was undressing, he saw that Atrakovksy was smiling at him from the next bed. And he smiled, too, thinking how silly he must have looked sneaking in.

"Captain," he whispered, "pull my sleeve."

Atrakovsky sat up on the bed, his bare feet flat on the floor. After his last attack, he was very weak and almost never got up. The doctors had run in, put a screen around his bed, separated him from the rest of the room. He lay there, all cold, rarely opening his dull eyes.

"Don't strain, just hold it," Tretyakov said. "I'll get out of it myself." He got out, caught his breath, adjusted his bandage.

"Thanks."

"Want a smoke?"

"I'm dying for one. Finished all of mine."

With a weak hand Atrakovsky felt under his pillow and began putting on his robe.

"Let's go, I'll stand with you. I'm not sleeping anyway."

"Why aren't you sleeping? Are you in pain?"

"Thinking."

"Thinking!" Tretyakov smiled. He kept wanting to smile for some reason. "We'll think after the war's over. Look at

Starykh, he's sleeping like a saint. He doesn't think about anything." Starykh slept on his stomach, his hand reaching the floor. And it didn't bother him the least that they were whispering near him. He turned on his side, the bed creaked—he wasn't tall, but he was built like a rock. His white cast showed beneath the blanket.

"I slept like that at the front," Tretyakov said. "I slept wherever I could. It seems amazing now. Our commander slept in a dugout and a shell exploded under it. The ground was swampy, the shell went deep, and there wasn't enough powder to throw up the dirt, just enough to shake up the beds. He didn't wake up. In the morning, he saw that the dirt-shelf beds were bulging. That's how I slept. Here there are no fleas, but I feel bites and pricks all night. Did anyone miss me?"

"No."

Tretyakov put his clothes under the mattress and got into his robe. "Shall we go?"

They went over by the operating room, to the far window. From there they could see the lights of the train station, the lights on the tracks. The window was like all the others, but for some reason all the most honest conversations took place there. He had sat there with Sasha, too.

Tretyakov had not smoked in so long that it made his lips numb. He stared at the window and smiled, not aware of Atrakovsky watching him.

The man had seen Tretyakov brought in and observed the boy coming back to life before his eyes. The boy's cheeks were bluish now from being out in the cold, but he was smiling and happy. Nevertheless, even when he smiled, there was something serious in his eyes. They had seen things. He pitied the boy and envied him.

In 1941, when Atrakovksy was wounded and taken prisoner by the Germans, he saw their entire column from a hilltop. The rain had stopped, the evening sun was bright, and the light was so strong it felt as if life was burning out.

And the entire length of road was filled with Russian prisoners guarded by submachine guns. And where the Germans were taking them, in the middle of the swamps, were hundreds, maybe thousands of people, so many he couldn't see the ground under them; just heads, heads, heads, like fish roe. Boys like Tretyakov, with their heads shaved. How many of them could still be alive now? It was then that he understood how little a single human life meant in this war. A life that by itself was priceless lost its value when multiplied by thousands, hundreds of thousands, millions. But these insignificant lives, these people who could fight to the last in combat, in prisoner-of-war camps were reduced to squabbling over rotten leftovers, were shot at by the well-fed young German guards, shot at for fun from behind the barbed wire because it was allowed; these people, and none others, were special and were the unique power that could overcome anything. With what sacrifice and readiness that power rose up at every fatal moment when destruction threatened the homeland.

There was a pilot with him in the POW camp, a boy like Tretyakov, a bit older. He had been shot down right over his target. Without hesitation he aimed his plane at a railroad bridge, ready for certain death. But he survived, thrown aside by the blast. He died from an infection, but to the last minute he dreamed of escaping. And if he had escaped, he would have had to prove that he hadn't betrayed anyone, hadn't been a traitor, just as Atrakovksy had been forced to, and he too would have been left with an ineradicable stain. Nothing hurt Atrakovsky in the prison camp; the enemy is the enemy, he didn't expect anything good from them. His heart was a stone there. But when your own people don't believe you, nothing is more painful.

Muffled by the double panes, the train whistle blew. Passing the station, a freight train whizzed by, two locomotives, pulling it, cars and platforms appearing and disappearing. It was headed for the front. When the train vanished and the tracks were empty, the two men looked at each other with the same look in their eyes. And for the first time Tretyakov noticed that Atrakovsky was not old, he was just very thin, a skeleton.

Once, when they were changing the linens and Atrakovksy pulled off his shirt, exposing his backbone, arched and sharp, Tretyakov saw his arm, the one he was now leaning against the windowsill. Mashed, full of horrible holes, covered with shiny, wrinkled skin—as if huge hunks of flesh had been torn away—the arm the man had fought with, winning the Order of the Red Banner, his "pass into life," as he had called it.

"We'll look back on this time," Atrakovsky said, and his eyes shone. "Whoever lives will remember it. Are you drawn back there already?"

"Yes!" Tretyakov was amazed that the captain was expressing his own thoughts. "Back there, when it's really tough, you think, I wish I'd get wounded! And here . . ."

Atrakovsky regarded him as a father does a son. "You can't lift your head there, but your soul stands at its full height."

"That's why I liked commanding my platoon," Tretyakov interrupted. He wanted to talk too. "You get away from the battery, and there's no one above you. The closer to the front lines, the freer you are."

"A great freeing of the spirit comes through a great catastrophe," Atrakovsky said. "Never has so much depended on each of us. That's why we'll win. And it won't be forgotten. A star fades, but its magnetic field remains. People are like that too."

They stood at the window a long time, and even in their silences they spoke. Looking into the boy's eyes, Atrakovsky read Tretyakov's future in them.

21

Oleg Selivanov peeked into the ward and beckoned to Tretyakov to come out into the corridor. "Let's go!"

"Did you bring it?"

"They're unloading it now." Oleg's windburned face was red, and golden stubble showed in the pores of his thick skin. "Hurry it up. I spoke with the hospital chief, they'll let you out."

They walked down the street in step, their heels ringing on the frozen snow. The winter day smelled of spring.

This was Tretyakov's first walk in town in broad daylight: Oleg Selivanov, eyeglasses shining, strapped in belts and bandoleers, was his convoy and his protection.

"How did you manage this, Oleg?"

He smiled. "You think just because I'm here I know everything? I don't know a thing. Or how to do anything. Luckily, I ran into a man who did, and he offered to take care of it."

"Thank you, Oleg."

"I feel good about it myself, if you must know." They were walking quickly, talking as they walked, their breath coming in bursts of steam. This taught him never to make promises to himself. Seeing Oleg off the other time, Tretyakov had sincerely hoped never to see him again. He hadn't known he'd seek Oleg out himself and be glad when they brought him to the hospital.

"Oleg," he had said, because there was no one else to ask, "I need a carload of firewood." Oleg's eyes grew rounder than his glasses.

"Volodya, where will I get it? A whole carload at that."

"I don't know." But they both knew that he had to find out. Of their entire class, of all the gang, Oleg was the only one who stayed in the rear. Tretyakov wouldn't have asked for himself, but he couldn't leave Sasha to gather coal under trains. He had no doubts that Oleg could do it if he set his mind to it. People going through the medical board in the third year of the war valued their lives more than a load of firewood, and Oleg was secretary of the board. "He has the seal," the hospital administrator explained. The seal didn't mean anything to Tretyakov, but from the tone in which it was said, he understood: People's fates were in his hands.

Oleg now was bursting with pride. It was a good experience, doing a good deed for someone else. When they reached the house, out of breath from their fast pace, there was a mountain of six-foot logs on the snow in front of the shed, and Sasha was tugging at them. She looked up with a birch log in her arms and smiled at them with joy.

"I thought it was for Faya. I called her, and they read the note and said it was for me."

"You could have sent them away."

"Have they left?" Oleg asked.

"They were in a hurry. They dumped it quickly, and wouldn't even take money. 'What do we want with money? How about some alcohol?' Where would I find alcohol?" Sasha walked toward them, shaking wood shavings from her mittens. "Volodya, I don't understand."

"Here, I'd like you to meet Oleg Selivanov." He pushed Oleg forward. "A great and all-powerful man. We were in the same class. It's all his doing." Sasha offered her hand, warm from the mitten. Oleg grew embarrassed and began cleaning his glasses.

"And they're almost all birch!" Sasha exclaimed. "Look how many birch logs!"

"We won't look." Tretyakov took off his belt and looped it over his shoulder. He saw that the logs had made much more of an impression on Sasha than Oleg had. "We'll cut them up and stack them in the shed."

The neighbors had a sawhorse in the shed. Faya put on her shawl and brought them a two-handled saw. She came out again and brought them an axe. She liked it when things were working well, and was glad to help her neighbor. They trampled down the snow around the sawhorse, and started with a big log.

"Come on, Sasha!"

When the first sawed-off round fell on the snow, Oleg Selivanov started chopping. In his coat, belt, bandoleer, he swung the axe over his head, and his glasses fell from his nose. He sat down on a log, stunned by his clumsiness, poking his broken lens and holding it up to the light. Sasha and Volodya sawed.

White curls of wood shot out from under the saw; they fell on Sasha's felt boots and on the bottom of Tretyakov's coat, on his boots. They made a yellowish layer underfoot, on the snow, and the smell of cut wood filled the air.

Sasha got red, and untied her shawl, and the hair near her blazing cheeks curled softly.

"Are you tired?"

She shook her head. "No."

The sharp saw moved smoothly. She pulled it toward herself in two mittened hands, and then tossed off the mittens; it was hot. Behind her, like smoke that had not pulled away from the earth, stood birch trees covered with hoarfrost, shrouded in silence.

It grew warmer by midday, a cloud formed, and snow fell heavily, swirling around them. The birch smell grew stronger, as if it were coming from the snow.

From the station came the racing pounding of wheels, steadily, rhythmically falling, carrying in the air. Locomotive smoke filled the air. Soon he would be on a train, and the wheels would be clacking beneath him. He looked at Sasha—this is how he would remember her.

A face, white in the black kitchen window, had appeared several times.

"That's Mother!" she shouted over the noise of the saw. "I brought her home yesterday. She's so strange, keeps asking questions. And she walks around the house as if she doesn't recognize anything." Sasha took a breath. "She had pneumonia there, it seems. No one told me."

A white hand waved in the window. Sasha ran into the house, and Oleg took her place. Then they sat down on the logs to have a smoke. The snow had stopped. The sun was shining again. Tretyakov looked at the number of logs left and tried to figure if they had the strength to finish. He put his hand on Oleg's knee. His hand seemed puffy.

"Thanks, Oleg."

"Don't be silly. I just wish you had told me sooner."

Sasha brought them drinks and went back into the kitchen. She came out waving the long sleeves of a jacket. It came down to her knees.

"Faya gave me this!" she said, laughing, rolling back the quilted sleeves.

She looked lovely in it, and Tretyakov saw the lovesick look in Oleg's eyes.

Sasha carried more wood to the shed, and they sawed it. Only when every last log was sawed and put away, when the sawhorse was back in the shed and Sasha had picked up the small pieces of wood and bark from the snow, did they pick up the saw and the axe and all go inside.

Tretyakov looked back from the porch. The area in front of the shed was clear. They had done it all in one shot. Their boots noisily scraping, they entered the kitchen single file, leaving their tools outside the door.

"You're not workers, you're saints!" Faya said, and stood swaying, hands folded on her belly, blocking half the kitchen. He saw a thin old woman wearing Sasha's shawl standing by the stove. Sasha hugged her.

"This is my mother!" she said, and looked quickly to see his reaction. Then she said, "Mama, this is Volodya."

"Volodya," her mother repeated, covering her mouth with her hand, embarrassed by her missing front tooth. Her hand was white, bloodless; it even looked cold with its white nails.

"They cut Mama's hair for some reason," Sasha said, fluffing up her hair around her ears. "Mama's braids were longer than mine, and she let them cut her hair. I wouldn't have let them do it, had I known."

"Take off your coats," Sasha's mother said. "Everything's ready. Sit down at the table. Sasha, show them where to hang up their coats."

In the kitchen all the light of the sun setting over the snow now fell on the table, on the old, patched tablecloth, pink in the glow. The deep bowls shone pink.

Faya did not join them and went to her room. Sasha's mother took each plate to the stove to fill it and placed the steaming cabbage soup in front of each of them. The soup, without meat or butter, made with frozen cabbage leaves and potatoes, was tasty and aromatic. All the time they spoke and ate, Tretyakov felt the mother's eyes on him. She looked at him, added soup to the bowls, and looked at him. Oleg was upset and sad; the sun shone on his cracked lens. And because he was upset, he didn't notice that he was the only one eating the bread. He kept taking it, crumbling it on the tablecloth, and eating it.

The birch-tree tops showed through the window. The highest branches glowed bright red, while the trunks looked lilac in the transparent raspberry light. A train went by, the puffs of smoke moving above the sheds, and the light trembled over the table.

The sun was setting, the day was fading, the walls grew darker, and it was hard to make out the faces. But he still felt the mother's eyes on him.

It was dark by the time he and Sasha had walked Oleg home and were headed back toward the hospital. She asked, "Did you really like my mother?"

"You look like her," he said.

"You can't even imagine how much we're alike! When she had her braids, she looked young. Everyone took us for sisters. They couldn't believe she was my mother. She came back from the hospital like that. Old. I can't look at her."

They stood by the gate. The wind swirled snow around his boots and made his coat flap. He blocked Sasha from the wind, warmed her hands in his, and mentally bid her farewell.

"Mama," he wrote that evening, bent over the windowsill where he usually watched the train station and the departing trains, "forgive me for everything. Now I know how hard I made life for you. But I didn't realize it then, only now."

His mother once said to him in an angry moment, "You don't understand what it means in our day for someone to take the wife of an arrested man. And with two children at that. You don't understand what kind of a man would do that!"

"I don't need to be taken!" he had replied then. "I don't need anyone to take me!" And he dropped out of school to go to a technical school, where he would get a scholarship. He wanted to move to the dormitory, too, but they only took people from out of town. He now realized that he had been cruel. And he thought that if his father was alive and did return, he would understand and forgive, too. And suddenly, at the end of the letter, he wrote, "Take care of Lyalya!"

22

In the cloud of steam that blanketed the platform, women ran along the length of the train, calling their children in loud voices, climbing up on the steps. The conductors struck them on their fingers.

"Where are you going? There are no seats!"

"Volodya, Volodya! *This* car!" cried Sasha. She had picked up the station panic.

The woman conductor pushed her bosom against him. "It's full, don't you see?"

Tretyakov tossed his field bag over her head into the train and saw that someone caught it. People were running past, pushing and shoving.

"I'll write, Sasha. As soon as I get the field post office number, I'll write to you." He jumped up on the step of the moving train and moved the conductor aside with his shoulder.

Sasha walked alongside the steps, waving to him. Everything was flashing before her and she lost sight of him.

"Sasha!"

She looked past him, unable to find him. He jumped back down on the platform, embraced her and kissed her hard. Officers in fur vests jumping out of the train station looked at them as they ran by and leaped into the train. He ran with Sasha; she pushed him away.

"Volodya, hurry! . . . You'll miss the train!"

The train was picking up speed. He jumped on. People left behind on the platform were still trying to reach the train. Sasha ran alongside, falling behind, shouting something. The train curved, Sasha ran off to one side, waved one last time—and she was gone. The taste of her tears was on his lips.

The conductor, without looking, pushed against the stragglers with her back, forced them inside, shut the metal door with the sooty window. It was quieter. Someone handed him his bag.

"From the hospital, Comrade Lieutenant?"

Tretyakov looked carefully at the speaker. "Yes."

"In a long time?"

He looked again, embarrassing the man with his look. He heard the words, but understood them later. He was seeing Sasha.

"Yes. Since fall." He took out his tobacco pouch. "Anyone got a newspaper?"

They let him tear off a column. Tretyakov poured in the tobacco and passed around the pouch. As the new man in the car, it was his treat. The pouch was a war trophy, made of rubber. When you let go of the mouth, it screwed itself up like a stopper. The tobacco did not dry out or lose its taste; it stayed moist and smoked well. Starykh had given it to him as a farewell gift.

The pouch made the rounds—everyone admired it—and returned to him. Everyone lit up at once. The wheels pounded beneath them, shaking them up. By now Sasha was on her way home; he could see her walking alone.

They finished smoking. Tretyakov tossed the bag over his shoulder and, with a nod, pushed the door into the car. The air was thick. He went down the aisle, swaying with the swaying floor. There were people on the lower berths, the upper berths, and on the luggage rack. It was crowded. Since the beginning of the war every spot was always taken. He found a spot over the window, where the heating pipe

142

passed near the ceiling. He threw his bag on the luggage rack, climbed up, and lay on his side. That was the only way to fit. Holding on to the ceiling with one hand and then the other, he took off his coat, spread it under him, and put the bag under his head. There. At night he would fasten his belt around the heating pipe, and he could sleep without falling off.

He lay there, thinking. All the tobacco smoke rose up to the ceiling. The stuffiness made him sleepy.

When he woke up there was light on the ceiling. It was the setting sun, burnishing each plank. He unbuttoned his collar, wiped his neck, sweaty from sleep. Then he had a sinking feeling. He was far away now. And nothing could be changed.

He carefully climbed down and walked along the train. People were smoking, talking, eating; their expressions flashed as he walked past.

On the metal platform between the cars a woman was giving two children something to drink from a mug. Her packages were blocking the door to the next car. She looked up at him in fright—would he chase them away?—and saw that he was unwilling to light up, though he had his pouch out.

"Smoke! The children are used to it," she said.

The children seemed to be the same age; their wet lips glistened the same way.

"Yes. They re used to it," an old man said in a weak voice. It was only then that Tretyakov noticed him; the beard and hat amid the bags and parcels. He understood and gave the old man a smoke.

"Why waste tobacco on him?" The woman said, prettier now that she was smiling.

This train was not for civilian passengers. But after every station they were in the cars, on the platforms; they had to travel and they managed to get on somehow. This woman was traveling with her children, her things, and the old man, who was clearly a burden. After he lit up, he coughed until he turned blue, until tears came to his eyes, shivering. After each inhalation he checked his cigarette to see how much he had left.

At the other door a pilot and a young woman stood face to face. He was telling her about an aerial battle, his arms tracing flights in the air; the woman followed with her eyes, her face filled with delight and horror. The pilot was handsome, his hair was cropped short in the back, his neck was in a tight high collar, and along the white trim, as if it were a white thread, holding tight, crawled a large louse. Tretyakov didn't know how to tell the pilot so that the woman wouldn't notice.

The conductor came out with a rolled-up flag; the smell of the toilet came from the car. They were coming to a station.

"Can't you get them into the car?" Tretyakov said softly, his eyes indicating the children and the window covered with frost. The mother heard him and flapped her hands at him.

"Oh, no! We're fine here! Couldn't be better!"

The conductor unfurled the sooty flag with her hand.

"Don't you feel sorry for yourself?" the conductor asked and gave Tretyakov a grim look. "I feel sorry for you. This whole war I've been taking boys like you to the front—and it's always just one way."

23

The campfire hissed, the melted soil around it dried, and the steam and smoke from the damp sticks stung their eyes. The sooty battery soldiers hadn't slept in two days. They sat, backs to the wind, smearing the dirty tears on their cheeks with their arms while their cold contorted fingers reached toward the fire. The wet snow flew at an angle into the campfire, onto their backs and hats.

Filling a bucket with snow, Kytin took it to the fire. There was more smoke than fire.

"Fomichev!" he shouted. "Give it another splash."

The motor-pool driver came over, his oily felt boots sloshing through the melted snow. Everything he wore was stained with oil and gasoline. He splashed gasoline onto the fire from a crumpled metal pail. It flared up and the heat hit their faces. Those who were asleep woke up and stared at the fire.

Protecting himself with his glove, Kytin sidled up to the fire. Fomichev waited with the rest of the gasoline. A look at his soaked felt boots made Tretyakov think he should change his shoes. He was sitting on an ammo box, his body racked with coughs. His forehead, chest, stomach muscles— everything hurt from the cough, and it hurt his watering eyes to look at the fire. He had been wet and icy at the front so many times but had never caught cold! And now, after spending time between clean sheets at the hospital, he got sick the first time out.

He pulled off a damp boot with difficulty, unwrapped the foot cloth. His bare foot was whipped by the wind, a chill went up his spine, and he felt feverish all over. He wanted to cover his head with his coat, breathe on his numb fingers, shut his eyes.

The battery commander came over to the fire. He was new, from a different unit—Captain Gorodilin. They said that he had been the deputy chief of staff of the regiment and that he couldn't forget his former position; the battery wasn't high enough for him. That was why he kept everyone at a distance—both the platoon commanders and the soldiers. He spoke only with the master sergeant. But soon they figured it out. The battery commander had no self-confidence. No matter how sternly he frowned or how he yelled, they followed his orders, even sensible ones, reluctantly. That's the way it always is: Uncertainty in the order gives rise to even greater uncertainty in its execution. Everyone kept thinking about Povysenko: Now *he* had been a battery commander! He didn't give orders. He'd just say something, and everyone rushed to do it.

But Povysenko had been wounded just before New Year's and was no longer with the regiment. There were several new people in Tretyakov's platoon. There had been a new junior lieutenant to replace him, but he had been killed before the men had time to learn his name. Tretyakov was welcomed back by the men as if they had fought half the war together. The word went out, "Our lieutenant is back." He was touched and felt he had come home.

The battery commander took a glowing branch and lit his cigarette with it. They could tell what he was going to say. The advance had been going on for several days now, and the rear had fallen behind. Food, fuel, ammunition—everything was behind them. Stuck vehicles were all along the

146

roads in the wet snow. They would try to haul them out, only to have them sink deeper in the mud. In their artillery division, only two batteries out of three were left. Two guns, two tractors, seventeen rounds—that was their whole division, hurrying to catch up with the front.

The battery commander finished his smoke and tossed the branch back into the fire under the bucket.

"Planning to eat?" He squinted and listened to a rumbling noise to his left. "You won't have dinner. We have orders to take firing positions. Platoon commanders, come here."

Kytin was still looking into the pail of snow. Then he angrily dumped it onto the fire. Steam swirled up from the hissing black coals. It scalded the battery commander, who turned red, his trim white mustache standing out in contrast.

"No back talk!"

But no one was talking. Exhausted, beyond feeling sorry for themselves after two days without sleep and almost no food, they were angry with the commander for not letting them make dinner and angry with each other, the way they should have been angry with the war.

Tretyakov was pulling on his damp boot when Lavrentyev, commander of the rifle platoon, hurried by. He was rushing toward the battery commander with a frightened look and slipping on the wet snow, which made it look as if he were crouching. The skirts of his coat were buttoned in front to his belt, the way infantrymen do. Like a woman, thought Tretyakov, and got up. He went over to Gorodilin and spoke quietly, so that the men wouldn't hear.

"Commander, you have to let the men make their dinner." He coughed.

"Are you sick?" Gorodilin asked, grimacing. The best way to make a subordinate shut up is to point out his defects.

"I'm not sick. I'm fine. The men haven't had a hot meal in a long time."

He saw that Gorodilin would not change his order. The

less confident a commander is, the more inflexible he is, that's the rule. He wouldn't take advice, and he wouldn't rescind his order, afraid to lose authority.

"Get out your map," Gorodilin said.

Tretyakov took out his map.

The battery commander couldn't resist. "By the way, I haven't had any hot food either, as you might have noticed. And I'm fine."

If you're a commander you don't eat at all, but you make sure your men eat, thought Tretyakov.

"Here we are. Here's the enemy, approximately! Go to the infantry and find out which firing company is in front. Establish communications. Is that clear?"

"Yes sir."

"Take four scouts with you."

Tretyakov saluted.

They crossed a dale. The snow had been blown into here, and it was melting in some places. They pulled boots full of water from deep holes. The meadow rose ahead of them. They could hear shooting in the distance. There were no planes; pilots were grounded in visibility like this, playing dominoes in their boredom. The airfields must be snowed in, too. No takeoffs, no landings.

At the crest, in thin bushes, they lay down to look around. They smoked. No matter how hard Tretyakov peered through his red, swollen eyes, he could not see the infantry nearby. No trenches, no dugouts, no traces at all. Just a snowy field, disappearing in the damp distance.

Coughing tore at his throat again.

"Eat some snow," Obukhov suggested.

"A fine idea!"

Tretyakov inhaled smoke and held it in his throat. He could hear melting snow falling with a rustle from branches.

"Look!" he said to Obukhov.

Midges swarmed in the air above the bush.

"They're awake, they sense the warmth," Obukhov said. "The snow smells of spring."

"I can't smell a thing right now."

They spoke in low voices, listening all the time. Obukhov dug up some of last year's frozen grass under the snow and put a clump in his mouth, like scallions. He craved greens. Tretyakov's inflamed throat felt the icy cold and a chill was going through his whole body.

"Will we bump into the Germans, Comrade Lieutenant?" Obukhov asked. "It doesn't look like there's any infantry ahead."

"No, it doesn't."

Tretyakov pulled the strap from his shoulder and held his submachine gun. He signaled Obukhov to go separately. He was right to have taken not four scouts, only one. They were very visible against the snow; if the Germans got close they'd get all four.

From a trembling, wavering haze rose last year's haystack, with a melting snow cap on top. If the Germans had a machine gun under the stack . . . But there were no footprints around. They went closer.

They were shot at when the bare wet poplars of a farm appeared in the gray mist. Traces of bullets flashed at them. The Germans used tracer bullets in the daytime too. They lay in the snow, but the machine gun kept shooting. They crawled far apart from each other. Tretyakov shot a few times, just to draw their fire. Fire came from two sides. Then came a mortar shell. They waited. Then they jumped up and ran back to the haystack. The machine gunner sent fiery arcs after them.

"I told you the infantry wasn't in front!" Obukhov had brightened with the danger.

"Stupid Germans, they should have let us get closer." His chest had cleared, and his cold seemed to have disappeared.

"Just wait, those Germans will attack," Obukhov promised.

"If they have the what for."

"They do."

They were more cheerful going back and the road seemed shorter.

The men were digging foxholes for the guns. Battery Commander Gorodilin listened to them suspiciously, repeating, "But where's our infantry?" He made them tell it again, where they went, where the shots came from. He couldn't believe that their battery and their heavy guns were stopped here without any cover, almost without ammunition, and right up ahead were the Germans.

The damp, raw day grew darker. They made the crest where they had smoked in the bushes an observation point and set up a line in the twilight. The scouts took turns battering the ground with a shovel, took turns being on lookout. It got dark. The fog thickened, covering the field, and soon they could see nothing.

The frozen earth did not respond well to the shovel. They made a small breastwork, broke branches, and dragged over some hay. They sat and listened. Tretyakov felt his fever rising. His back was chilled, and at times he could not control the shivering.

It was very dark when he heard footsteps and the heavy breathing of several people. When they came closer, he recognized Gorodilin and the division commander. Two scouts were with them.

The fourth battery had reached them and was taking firing positions. The division commander asked what they heard here. He asked questions and looked at their faces.

"Well, battery commander," he said to Gorodilin, "you and I will stay here till morning." He sent Tretyakov back to the firing positions so that he could rest in the warmth at the farm. He added. "In the morning you'll relieve us. That's the right way to do it," he said, and nodded to himself.

24

That night was a long one. Tretyakov drank half a pail of water but his fever didn't drop. His chapped lips cracked and bled. He felt delirious. He went outside several times. The fog made it hard to breathe.

In the morning he awoke wet and weak. But everything seemed clearer and brighter. Lavrentyev, stripped to the waist, was washing by the wall, sloshing water under his arms, water dripping down his chest and stomach. Tretyakov sat on the dirt floor. His face had grown taut and his eyes hollow overnight, he could feel it. He thought he should make some tea. Suddenly there was a soldier in the doorway.

"Tanks!"

Soldiers ran past the door. The sound of tanks was deafening outside. A soldier running in front of him slipped in the wet snow and was getting up, scared. He made a run for it to the side.

"Where do you think you're going?!" Tretyakov shouted, his voice a whiplash. "Back!" Bending lower under the shout, the soldier ran to the foxhole. The gun squad was there, unwrapping the heavy guns, making calculations.

"There they are! There!" Paravyan called and pointed from behind the shield. The fog lifted low above the ground, giving about a hundred fifty meters of visibility.

Rising behind the trees, armored transport moved down

the road; their dull heavy bodies were like concentrated fog. "One, two, three . . ." Paravyan counted them. The tanks were moving into a flank position.

"Ready!" yelled Tretyakov, ending his moment of bewilderment, and jumped up on the breastwork.

"Ready!" echoed from the other gun. The tanks kept rolling over the hill, moving in the fog, behind the trees.

"Seventeen, eighteen, nineteen," Paravyan counted to himself.

"Warning—one corps!" Tretyakov said from above to the gunlayer and peered more intently, shaking his head. Something was bothering him, slapping his cheeks—he was still wearing the hat with earflaps he had slept in. He pulled it off his head, impatiently. To have something to do he pressed it to his chest to tie the strings. He stared at the road, breathing heavily, his head bare. His fingers shook and he couldn't tie the strings.

He could already see how short this battle would be. Their gun had nine shells; the other one had eight. And the tanks kept coming over the hill. "Fire!" The earth trembled underfoot. Fire flew over the road, and a tree shuddered in the fog as it fell. Fire flew up a few more times, in the field, beyond the road.

The gunlayer was in a hurry, nervous. "I'll get him!" Bullets struck the shield and hissed in the mud. Fiery traces pelted the gun from all sides. The tanks had turned from the road and were headed for the battery. They crawled out of the fog, which dissipated into tatters before them, and each one sparkled fire, hitting low on the field. You could see submachine gunners jumping out of the tanks, then running in a crowd behind them. They were shooting too.

"Chabarov!" Tretyakov shouted, jumping down into the foxhole. "Gun off their infantry! Don't hurry. Aim. Don't hurry." He kept count in his mind: five shells left. Five shots. The second gun fired. Somewhere behind them, the fourth battery was firing. That meant the Germans had broken through there, too. There was a low howl. A mine! The gunlayer's back shuddered. Without taking his eyes from the viewfinder, still taking aim, he cringed, feeling that flying mortar shell. Sweat poured down his cheek; murky drops trembled on his chin. The mine was still howling above them when the gun went off. Tretyakov, from behind the shield, saw the front tank, its gunners jumping over the side, blow up with blue fire.

And then several shells exploded at the same time. When Tretyakov got up, he was covered in mud. Someone was moving blindly between the side plates, groaning. The gun squad was running from the second gun. It stood in the foxhole, its side plates spread out, aiming at the field, but they were running. Among them, taller than the rest, was Lavrentyev, his coat open. A flat explosion came, scattering and hitting the runners. Lavrentyev grabbed his back, bent over as he ran, fell.

More tanks were coming from the farm, from Kravtsy, going to the rear of the battery. The shed in which they had spent the night collapsed, falling forward. A tank rumbled under it, turning its turret, logs rolling from it; the thatched roof slipped onto it. The abandoned gun in the foxhole jumped up, as if it had shot on its own, and settled in the smoke of the explosion. Bent low under a stream of bullets, Tretyakov saw the fear on the faces of the scattering people. He had to get the bolt from the gun.

He didn't have time to shout; an explosion sent them all to the dirt. Lying flat in the mud, he listened to the shells flying overhead.

Tretyakov leaned on his elbows. "Run to the ravine! To the trees! There's snow. . . ." He fell before another explosion. Thunder. He looked up. "To the trees! The snow is deep there! Everybody, go there!"

A hit on the breastwork. Tretyakov lay with his eyes shut. A whine overhead. He jumped up.

"Paravyan! Take the bolt! Hurry!" Paravyan was standing

in the foxhole, one hand on the gun, his face turning blue. And in his side . . . Tretyakov saw it and didn't believe his eyes. In his side, bright red, seeping, an exposed lung breathed in and out. It was breathing, but Paravyan was suffocating without air, gulping it with his dying, gaping mouth. Someone's trembling hands got the bolt. Nasrullaev. His gentle, fearless eyes looked at him. "Run, Eldar!" Holding the heavy bolt to his stomach, Nasrullaev ran.

Paravyan sat on the ground. His face was covered with tears and sweat. His eyes were glazing. Kneeling, tense, Tretyakov poured submachine-gun shells into his pocket. Bullets whizzed overhead. He put the submachine-gun strap over his head, and bent low, he ran from the foxhole. People were running all over the field. Looking around, falling, jumping up, running. A tank came up on Nasrullaev from the side. He dropped the bolt and ran. A round of tracer bullets cut him down. Flat on his face, he tried to get up. Tretyakov did not see the tank run over him, but the inhuman scream seared his heart.

He ran under the bullets, panting, feeling his legs grow weak. He needed air. It grew dark before his eyes, and still the fresh layer of snow beckoned. Finally he was no longer running, he was walking on bending legs, sucking in air with burning lungs. He fell facedown in the snow. An engine roared toward him from the sky.

25

The German counterattack in the region of Apostolovo during the great spring advance of 1944 in the south Ukraine could not change a thing—neither the course of the war nor the course of history. It did temporarily slow the advance in that sector, but it meant nothing in the larger scope of the events. But each of the people who fought off that blow directed at them had only one life.

The unusually early spring a month before had turned the winter roads into black muck. Heavy machinery sank in them, the rear stretched out for five hundred kilometers, and the fuel they were bringing to the front got used up on the way. But the artillery got there, the tank corps made it there, and together they chased off the Germans who had broken through. The very German tanks that had passed the firing positions of the artillery, shooting and squashing living men, were now shot, burned, or found whole, stuck in the mud, abandoned in the fields.

On the third day they buried the dead. The snow had melted completely; there were dirty gray clumps only in the valley and in the trees where the wind had blown it. Puddles glistened in the sun, and among them, throughout the field, lay the dead. In overcoats soaked with water, in wet quilted shirts, stiff and bloated, they lay where death had found them. The field at the Kravtsy farm, where they sowed and harvested wheat from year to year and sent geese out to clean up every autumn, had become their last battlefield. And the living, slipping and sliding in the black mud, pulling their boots out of the muck with difficulty, walked around seeking and recognizing the dead.

Not far from the trees, about two hundred fifty meters from the spot where he fell in the snow and the last machine gun round passed over him, Tretyakov found Nasrullaev. He lay wearing boots covered with tons of earth, his squashed legs turned out unnaturally. He lay on his back, his quilted jacket pushed up over his bare belly to his chin. The wrist of the hand with which he shielded his eyes had stiffened. How he had screamed! The dark opening of his tortured mouth seemed to hold the silent echoes of that scream.

In the gun foxhole, between the opened side guards, sat Paravyan, his hatless head down on his chest. A dry stripe of blood went from his shaved nape to his ear. That meant he had still been alive and a German had come over and finished him off.

They picked up nineteen men on the field and buried them at Kravtsy. Lavrentyev was not among them. Many had seen him fall, holding his back. Maybe he was alive and the Germans had taken him prisoner, finishing him off somewhere along the way when the Russians put the heat on them.

The farm was filled with cars, horses, cannon, and soldiers running from yard to yard, campfires burning, kitchens smoking. A unit had arrived during the night. The air was filled with smoke, manure, gasoline. Someone called Tretyakov: "Comrade Lieutenant! Comrade Lieutenant!"

His platoon was sitting against the sun-warmed white wall of the house. An overturned carriage without wheels served as a table for the men, who sat on whatever was handy. A red-haired soldier with a carroty cheek color ran to the kitchen in the corner of the yard and brought back a bowl of soup. As he accepted the bowl, Tretyakov looked at his face. Light-brown, cheerful eyes under white lashes—it was Dzhedzhelashvili.

Only after he took a sip did he look to see what he was eating. Split-pea soup, thick and yellow. He closed his eyes and with the spoon toasted those who were no longer with them.

The whitewashed clay wall was pitted with bullet holes. Flies crawled along the wall. Emerald green, blue, slow after the winter, they were waking up in the spring sun. Why had people died? Why were they still dying? The war was over. It was *over*. It couldn't be changed now; he thought; we have won. But the ones who had started it were putting off the hour of their destruction, and they would keep sending more than one division to the front—infantry and tank— and people would keep killing each other and dying. Many more were doomed.

"Rama!" came the shout from the yard. The word passed through the entire farm. "Rama!" The two-fuselage German Fokke-Wolf scout plane circled high in the sky. The sun was blinding, and the white contrail glistened, but the plane itself was invisible except for the occasional aluminum glint. Everyone looked up from the ground. Tretyakov had seen many planes knocked down during the war, but never a rama. White puffs of smoke from the antiaircraft guns kept exploding, the sound coming much later.

Kytin jumped up on the carriage and shot his rifle. "Get down!" Chabarov said. "You think you're going to hit it?"

Tretyakov, tired of the noise of guns, said, "Get down!"

Kytin finished and laughed. "The guy's flying to his death."

Dzhedzhelashvili gathered the bowls and went to wash them in the puddle. He was the cook today. Everyone lit up. The sun was making them sleepy by the wall. Life for the living.

Chabarov started telling them how they dry-cure geese in the spring. "We have this kind of sun in March. There's still

157

snow on the ground, but the sun is bright, there's no dust, no flies. The geese are fat. Once you've had dried goose, you'll never want any other kind."

"Well!" Obukhov rushed him.

"What?" Chabarov didn't like to be interrupted.

"How do you dry-cure them?"

"It's easy. . . ."

The regimental commander's jeep appeared at the end of the street. And someone shouted, "The first division!"

"Too bad, sergeant," Kytin said, "we were just about to taste your geese."

A tractor engine roared in the next yard and a horse whinnied.

26

The moist warm winds from the sea drove spring north-ward, stripping snow from the vast plains, while in the south the roads dried out, and all along the right bank of the Ukraine the Russian troops advanced, on the way to liberate Odessa.

"Our life goes from war report to war report," his mother wrote. "We didn't have any letters from you, and it was like a stone on my heart. One day I heard your voice, heard it clearly. You were calling me. I was crazy all day. Then Lyalya came running in from the street. She had met the mailman. We were so happy, we read the letter together and couldn't understand it. I know you're fooling me, to keep me from worrying, but the battles must have been horrible. If they even mentioned that Apostolovo on the radio . . ."

And Sasha wrote, "I keep trying to convince Mother not to plant a garden this spring, but she's afraid not to. Faya says, 'Dig up the potatoes in the fall and then leave, without them!' But I can't, I just want to go home. The worst is behind us—we'll manage somehow. Oh! I forgot to tell you, Faya had a girl. So merry and so wise, she recognizes me already. And she doesn't look like either of them."

The warm wind ruffled the two pages in his hand, from the copybooks of Lyalya and Sasha. The sun, low over the steppe, warmed his back through his coat, and the winter hat made his head sweat. The tractor bounced and made him sleepy. His lids shut on their own.

Behind him, with his face to the sun, weapons commander Alavidze was singing something beautiful in Georgian that resembled a prayer. Maybe he was greeting the rising sun. Tretyakov turned around and saw Alavidze sitting on the gun while Dzhedzhelashvili and the bolt keeper, Kocherava, were walking alongside. Both were waiting for Alavidze to sing the melody.

The air shimmered over the steppe and the smoke of explosions rose soundlessly. When you're up in the tractor next to the engine, the war is strange and silent. With a shudder, Tretyakov woke up and refolded the letters from Sasha and his mother and sister. His letters must have crossed paths with theirs, traveling a long time through the field mails; they'd probably take Odessa before his letters reached them.

An abandoned German gun stood right by the road. For some reason the German cannon always looked more massive and heavier than the Russian. Covered with camouflage, the gun had gotten stuck in the mud and the Germans didn't have time to pull it out. And there was a German tank, too. This was the way the battlefields looked in 1941, but then the Germans were the winners, and they got to keep everything that had been shot down or abandoned. Now the Russians were winning.

Tretyakov put the letters away in his shirt pocket and took out a mirror in a leather case. The mirror was a fine one, nonbreakable, made of polished steel. Yesterday at sundown his scouts and the infantry had burst into a grove. Some German unit had been there. They'd left, abandoning everything: fuel in barrels buried in the ground, crates of canned goods. In the hay they found a keg of wine and an officer's uniform with an Iron Cross and this mirror in the pocket. He must have run away with only one prayer—to escape alive. But now, if he was alive, he must be sorry about the Iron Cross. They won't give him a new one.

Obukhov was playing with the Iron Cross, saying when he got home, he'd put it on the dog's collar.

Tretyakov took off his hat and put it on his lap. He looked at himself in the steel mirror and thought about Sasha, his mother, Lyalya, about Odessa and the Black Sea. He had never been there in his life. When the Red Army took Odessa, in about two days, he'd sleep! If someone gave the order, both sides would sleep without waking. But that doesn't happen in war. In war the loser is whoever can't take it. It was horrible to think of all he'd been through during these years, and he hadn't even started combat in 1941. Most of those who had fought in 1941 had been killed. That's who he really felt sorry for, the ones who had died when things looked so bad, they hadn't had a hope of victory.

In their letter, Mother and Lyalya congratulated him on his birthday. On April twenty-eighth he would be twenty. Once upon a time he used to think twenty-five was elderly. What had he been doing on his birthday a year ago? He was in training school, on guard duty. Guard duty was best at night, if it wasn't cold. You're all alone, the stars shining up above, and you think whatever you want to think about. Night is the only time your thoughts are free, but that's also when you sleep. During the daytime you don't have a second to yourself.

The tractor ride was bumpy, everything bounced in the mirror. His forehead flashed by, divided in half by his tan, then his hair, matted by the hat, then his chin. Above their heads, three fighter planes flew up into the sky. They could see everything going on down on earth. They could probably see the division stretched out in its march. It had been sent along with the motorized infantry and the light artillery to support the tanks. They could probably see the tanks up ahead in combat.

Last night they had entered a train station, and a German echelon was there. It had arrived with the wounded after the

161

Russian tanks had passed. The Germans ran to the different houses and hid in them, not letting the residents come out. The Russian infantry caught them in gardens and cellars. Some got shot, but many were still on the run, hiding out somewhere, and would try to get back to their troops in the next few nights.

Tretyakov dozed off on the tractor. When he woke up, something was happening on the road ahead. The division commander was on horseback. He was short, so he always tried to get up on something higher. The horse spun around, dancing, while the division commander pointed at something to the side. The tractors turned and hauled the guns across the field.

Tretyakov jumped down. Gorodilin was already running toward him, shouting from a distance.

A shell exploded in the field; he heard machine guns.

"What's happening?"

"We've been ordered to take a defensive position. Somewhere to the right the Germans are breaking through to their lines."

Tretyakov ran to the trucks, calling his men on the run. "Chabarov! Take the Ford-eight to those bushes!" He jumped up on the running board of the Zis. Obukhov and Kytin jumped in with the submachine guns from the other side. The Zis was old, with a wooden cab; it had been through half the war. Holding on to the door, bumping along on the running board, Tretyakov showed the way to the driver and looked over the area, trying to understand what was happening. He could see the battery spreading out. A few more explosions hit the field. They were hitting with the heavy artillery. Someone galloped by on a horse, leaving a cloud of dust.

Leaning over the driver, Tretyakov showed which way to go. He found a steep hill; that was the best place. The driver nodded; Tretyakov jumped off and ran back. The Ford was stuck. He hadn't gone a hundred yards when he heard submachine-gun fire. The truck had stopped. Obukhov had his gun out. Kytin was backing away from the truck as if avoiding something.

Tretyakov ran back to them, pulling out his handgun. He heard Obukhov, pale, finger on the trigger, shout: *"Hände hoch!"* He pointed with his submachine gun. *"Schnell, schnell!"* Seeing Tretyakov running toward them, he called joyously, "We almost ran them over! . . . They were lying there. . . . Almost crushed them!"

From the bushes came the Germans, hesitantly raising their hands. Tretyakov ran over, waved his gun at them, and chased them onto the field. Obukhov, Kytin, and the driver accompanied them. Scouts from another vehicle came over and checked the bushes.

"Where'd you get them?"

"They were right here."

"Almost ran them over."

"Right here, in the bushes?"

"I heard the shooting."

Fourteen Germans stood in the field, huddling together, trying to understand from the Russians' faces what awaited them. Fear crumpled their faces and erased all human expression from then. Chabarov flushed two others from the bushes and pushed and kicked them forward. The soldiers—some laughing, some with angry sparks in their eyes—waited. The Germans huddled anxiously. When the two reached the crowd, they got into it.

The German officer closest to Tretyakov, asking permission with a smile, lowered the one arm he had up—the other was heavily bandaged and in a sling—and got something from his field bag. He offered it to Tretyakov, babbling in his tongue. It was an artillery coordinate scale, not like the Russian ones. He kept pushing it at Tretyakov, nodding, nodding. Tretyakov instinctively moved away.

And suddenly, unexpectedly, he said in a loud voice, *"Nicht schiessen!"* and gestured that they would not be shot.

"Arbeiten! Nach Siberia!" The prisoners whispered among themselves. A German shell exploded nearby, and Tretyakov caught a snide, gloating smile from one of the prisoners. Chabarov took away their weapons and tossed their field bags and knapsacks into a pile.

"What should we do with all that?" he asked.

"What?" Angry with himself for the pity he had shown, he yelled so that everyone could hear, "How much horsepower do you think they make? Send them over to haul out the Ford."

Obukhov took the prisoners to the truck stuck in the mud. *"Arbeiten! Arbeiten!"* Not understanding right away what was wanted from them, the Germans surrounded the truck, not pushing it so much as pushing up against it. The soldiers shouted, "Come on! One, two! Hup!"

"Push! Push!"

Several explosions went off nearby. There were shells in the truck. If it was hit, the Germans pushing the truck and the soldiers commanding them would be nothing but a crater. The Germans pushed hard—one of them gave the orders, and the truck, its motor whining, almost made it to the top—then rolled back into the hole made by the spinning tires. They tried again, and the truck crawled up again. The soldiers rushed over to help. Everyone pushed. Shivering with the final effort, the truck rolled out and drove off, and they all ran after it for a few feet and then stopped. The smiles of common work well done left their faces.

"Kytin, Obukhov!" Tretyakov frowned, hearing another shell flying. "Take them to the rear. . . . Hurry it up!" He could tell that the shell was coming straight at them—the Germans heard it, everyone heard it. Two explosions, one after the other, blocked the truck. "Missed!" thought Tretyakov. And then a powerful blow, so hard he almost fell, tossed his left arm to the side. The prisoners screamed and scattered. A German lay contorted on the ground.

Tretyakov tried to raise his arm. It bent strangely and

hung in his ripped sleeve. When the pain began, things turned black. Squinting as if facing a fire, he clenched his teeth, trying to block the pain with pain. He saw Chabarov raise the butt of his submachine gun and a tall German reel away from it, covering his wounded face.

"Don't hit him!" Tretyakov shouted, and then, unable to fight it anymore, he started to groan.

About an hour and a half later the regimental surgeon had put Tretyakov's bones back together again and bandaged a section of tire to his arm. "Pull it higher," he said to the nurse who was putting it in a sling. "Like that." He admired his handiwork.

"Will they amputate my arm?" Tretyakov asked, unable to hide his fear.

The doctor smiled and said in a hearty manner, "You'll fight with that arm. You'll strike against Germans with that arm. Unless, of course, the war ends first."

"Thank you, doctor!" Tretyakov said. "It's the third time—and it's always this arm."

"The third will be the last. Things come in threes."

There weren't many wounded men, and all of them who could walk or crawl gathered on the sunny side of the house, waiting for transport. The doctor came out on the street too.

"The Germans?" he asked in surprise, listening to the nearby fire. "Are they breaking through in large numbers?"

Tretyakov heard the anxiety in his voice. "No, it doesn't look that way. But you should post guards for the night."

"Who?"

"The lightly wounded, the ones working here."

"The wounded have to get better," the doctor said.

"If they want to live, they'll do guard duty," said Tretyakov. He moved his shoulder and the pain seared him. Frowning, he watched a sergeant, a big healthy-looking fellow, come out of the house with his broom and sweep up the dust on the porch.

"And don't go easy on the slackers," he said to the doctor. "There are Germans around. Don't forget. They hide during the day. We almost ran some over, hiding in the bushes. But at night . . . There are plenty of guns lying around."

The first-aid wagon came by to load the wounded. Having decided to go on the next trip, Tretyakov sat on the porch steps with his coat over his shoulders, watching the paramedic, a young, pushy, and sharp woman. The driver jumped at the sound of her voice and hurried to obey her orders—and did it all wrong.

They loaded a wounded man. They put him in the straw at the bottom of the wagon and he moaned weakly. Men hobbled over on their own, trying to appear more pathetic than they were. Tretyakov took his cigarette lighter out of his pocket and lit up. The pain, dulled by novocaine, was not too bad. He could take pain like that; there would be worse pain ahead. They would be pulling the bandages from his fresh wound over and over until it started suppurating and the bandage would come off on its own. He could see the whole road he would have to travel. This time they would probably have to put his arm in a cast. He remembered the fellow in the train who dug out the maggots from his wound. That would be hard, when it began itching under the cast.

"Lieutenant! Come on!" The doctor was calling him to the wagon. Having prepared himself for the second trip, Tretyakov was happy. He came over.

"Get in," the doctor said. "Go." And he clapped him on the back carefully. Now that he was being sent to the rear, he felt a vague sense of guilt. He saw an elderly soldier sitting on the ground, his freshly bandaged leg stretched out before him. Tretyakov hesitated.

"Take him," he said quietly to the doctor. "I can walk."

The soldier heard him and came over, hobbling. He climbed in like a man claiming his due and yelled at the driver. "What are you waiting for? Let's go!"

"Don't give orders!" the paramedic shouted. She was sitting next to the driver. "Some commander . . . Watch it, or I'll send you packing!" He pretended not to hear. She moved over on the seat and said angrily to Tretyakov, "Sit down, Lieutenant. Everyone thinks he's in charge here."

He shook hands with the doctor, then looked around for the last time and got in. There. Life had come full circle again.

He was traveling with his back to the front. His platoon, the war—all that was left behind. The steppe was in a dusty haze of buds, the shadows of clouds flew over it, and hills or mountains rose like light-blue visions. And overhead, in the high, blinding sky, were row after row of fluffy white clouds.

Life was so wonderful, Lord, so glorious! It was like seeing it all for the first time. The shadow of a cloud rolled onto the horses' backs, and he felt it with his face and eyes closed in the sun.

"Slow down," he said to the driver. He got off and walked. His wound had been shaken up and it hurt again, but he knew that the wound would hurt for a while and then heal. Now his soul was at peace. The paramedic looked down at him with her sleepless eyes and moved over to his spot on the seat.

"Been at war long?" he asked, hoping to forget his pain by conversation.

She yawned. "Get a smoke." She was very young, with plump lips and a small mouth. She lit her cigarette from the driver's and coughed harshly on the first drag. The shadow of the cloud traveling over the steppe covered the valley. Something made Tretyakov wary. He did not know what it was, but he had the feeling of danger. Still feeling responsible and in command, he had watched the area, from above when he had been riding and now as he walked.

The horses stepped down the road, the driver urged them on with the reins, the wounded men smoked, and he walked alongside, holding on to the wagon. He looked up at the paramedic; he did not want to worry her needlessly.

The shadow moved; the sun lit up the valley. He had been worried for nothing.

"Been at war long?" Tretyakov asked, forgetting he had already asked.

"A long time," she said, her voice clear after the cough. "Everyone in my family is in the war. My big sister left right after her husband was killed. My brother, too. My mother and kid brother are at home, waiting for letters."

He walked along and continued to look up at her. What if she were Sasha? or Lyalya?

He never heard the machine gun. He was hit, knocked off his feet, and fell. It happened in an instant. Lying on the ground, he saw the horses run off down the slope, the young paramedic grab the reins from the driver, and he measured the growing distance separating him from them. He shot at random. More machine-gun fire followed. He had time to notice where the fire was coming from, to think that he was in a bad place, on the road, very visible, that he should roll into the gully. But at that instant something moved ahead of him. The world contracted. He saw it through the sight on his gun. There, on the muzzle of his gun, at the end of his extended arm, it moved again, something smoky gray rising against the sky. Tretyakov fired.

When the paramedic stopped the horses and looked back at the spot where they had been ambushed and where Tretyakov had fallen, there was nothing there. Only the cloud of an explosion rose from the earth. And row upon row of blindingly white clouds, given wing by the wind, floated in the heavens.

ABOUT THE AUTHOR

Grigory Baklanov was born in Voronezh, a very ancient Russian town in the steppes. He was graduated from the Gorky Institute of Literature in 1951, and has since written several short stories, articles, and books for children. He is also the editor of the prestigious journal *Znamia.*

FOREVER NINETEEN is based on Baklanov's own experiences as a youth on the front lines in World War II. Baklanov says that when he returned from the war, he wanted to tell everybody what it was like to have been there. But the more he wrote, the more he realized that it is impossible to relay the entire truth about the war within a single lifetime. FOREVER NINETEEN is a great testament both to the horror of war and to the greatness of the human spirit. This J. B. Lippincott edition is the first of Baklanov's books to be published in English in the United States.

Antonina W. Bouis was born in West Germany and educated in the United States. She holds degrees from Barnard College and Columbia University and has translated several books from Russian into English, including TESTIMONY: THE MEMOIRS OF DIMITRI SHOSTAKOVICH (Harper & Row); and WILD BERRIES by Yvegeny Yevtushenko (Morrow).